IN THE
GALWAY SILENCE

KEN BRUEN is one of the most prominent
Irish crime writers of the last two decades.
He received a doctorate in metaphysics,
taught English in South Africa, and then
became a crime novelist. He is the recipient
of two Barry Awards, two Shamus Awards
and has twice been a finalist for the Edgar
Award. He lives in Galway, Ireland.

KEN BRUEN

IN THE GALWAY SILENCE

A Mysterious Press book
for Head of Zeus

First published in the UK in 2018 by Head of Zeus Ltd

9 7 5 3 1 2 4 6 8

A catalogue record for this book is available from
the British Library.

ISBN (HB): 9781788545853
ISBN (XTPB): 9781788545877
ISBN (E): 9781788545860

Printed and bound in Great Britain by
CPI Group (UK) Ltd, Croydon CR0 4YY

Head of Zeus Ltd
First Floor East
5–8 Hardwick Street
London EC1R 4RG

WWW.HEADOFZEUS.COM

IN THE
GALWAY
SILENCE

This book is dedicated

to

Michael

Bec

Chris

Crowell

and

the wonderful Marie Lee, the essence of Grace,

alongside Leon, manager of Dubray's

Jean and Claude Renaud were twins.

Terrible twins.

Truly.

Les enfants terribles.

Their father was French and the mother from Galway.

On their eighteenth birthday they were given matching sports cars. That neither could drive was neither here nor there. The father had made a greedy fortune from one of the first hedge funds in Ireland and was cute enough to get out before the ax fell. He then invested in property and made more.

Instead of being jailed, he was made a Freeman of the City.

The twins on the said birthday went on a massive pub crawl.

Ingested

Ecstasy

Speed

Coke

Jack Daniel's.

And did it bring them any joy?

Nope.

Just added to their sense of entitlement. Barred from the clubs along Quay Street, they headed for the Spanish Arch,

I

seeking aggravation. Saw a man huddled in a wheelchair on the edge of the pier. Jean said,

"Let's fuck with the retard."

Claude shouted,

"Hey, spastic!"

Jean came up behind the chair as Claude came from the front. There was a moment of utter quiet, then the man lashed out and caught Claude in the groin, and then he was out of the chair and hit Jean with the flat of his hand in the throat. Moving quickly, he bundled them forcibly into the chair and secured them with duct tape, grabbed Jean's mouth and applied a liberal dose of superglue to his lips, then the same to Claude.

Finally, he took a sign wrapped in cellophane, attached it to the back of the twins, stood back, and, with a firm push, sent them into the water.

He waited as the water settled over their frenzied thrashing and, satisfied that he could read the sign, turned on his heel, strolled away.

The Irish
can abide
almost anything
save silence.

I was happy.

Unbelievable as that sounds.

I had endured just about every trauma there is and had reached the point of suicide, and then,

Things got worse.

I was friends with a nun, which is as unlikely as me being happy but true. I had helped her out some years back and we remained friends. She introduced me to her cousin Marion and we had clicked.

Were even considering moving in together. I had moved to a new apartment on the Salthill Promenade. Big spacious place with a view of the ocean that was astounding. I had been

Involved

Mired

Baffled

Over the past few years with a homicidal goth punk named Emily / Emerald. She had wreaked all kinds of murderous havoc until I had reluctantly taken her off the board.

Now get this.

She had left me a shit pile of money.

Go figure.

Thus the new pad and certainly a factor in my new view of the world.

For the zillionth time I had cut back on my drinking. Yeah, yadda, yadda. As Marion was fond of a drink, I was reasonably free from censure for the time being. Felt no need to mention the wee issue of Xanax. I had also stopped beating people in every sense.

Marion came with her own story: namely, a son.

Nine years old and the first time I met him I would like to think we bonded and shared warm days out at hurling matches.

Dream on.

Marion brought him to the GBC, my favorite restaurant as they still served old-fashioned grub and had no list of calories on the menu. The boy was small with blond hair and, fuck, a curled lip, from attitude rather than design. Before I could speak, he whined,

"Why couldn't we go to McDonald's?"

I put out my hand, said,

"I'm Jack."

He looked at my hand like it was diseased, scoffed,

"Who even shakes hands these days?"

I let that slide.

He sighed, said,

"I'm Jeffrey."

Least that is how I heard it. I said,

"Good to meet you, Jeffrey."

He raised his eyes to heaven, said,

"It's Joffrey."

I said,

"What?"

He looked at his mother, said,

"You tell him."

She said, with a tinge of mild hysteria,

"Like Joffrey in *Game of Thrones*?"

He stared at me, asked,

"You do know what that is?"

This asked with a world-weariness.

I said,

"Joffrey is the spoiled pup that gets poisoned."

I was sitting in Garavan's, black coffee with a base of Jay. Reading the latest horror from Trump. Le Pen was ranting in France and all of Europe in turmoil.

When you manage to grab the snug, it is implicit that you do not want company. A large man appeared before me, blocking the light, muttered,

"Taylor."

He was in that bad fifties range with streaks of stringy blond hair clinging precariously to the scalp. Disconcerting was the hint of baby powder from him. From a grown man it is just creepy.

I said,

"I'm busy."

He moved in front of me, launched a slew of photos on the table, said,

"I'm Pierre Renaud. You have heard of me."

Not a question.

I said,

"Nope."

There was a trace of accent in his speech, as with those for whom English is a second language.

He said,

"I received Man of the Year five years ago."

Before I could be scathing about that, he said,

"My beloved sons, look, murdered."

I looked at the photos and could make out two men bound and bloated in

A wheelchair?

I asked,

"Is that a notice pinned to one of them?"

"Yes."

I couldn't decipher it, asked,

"What is it?"

He took a deep breath, then said,

"Silence."

I tried,

"I am deeply sorry for your loss."

That seemed to seriously annoy him. He said,

"Your condolences mean nothing."

He produced a thick envelope, dropped it beside my empty glass, said,

"You will find who did this terrible thing and bring them to me."

I pushed the envelope aside, said,

"I won't."

This shocked him. He asked,

"You say no to me?"

I stood, pushed past him, got a refill, then back to the snug where he was still standing. I sat and went back to the paper. He leaned over, said,

"You will do this for me."

I was sorry for his loss but beginning to tire of the aggression, said,

"Go to the Guards."

He spat in contempt, said,

"Imbeciles."

I shrugged, not something I had ever done but felt it was at least Gallic. He gathered up the photos, said,

"*À bientôt.*"

Sounded a lot like

"Fuck you."

Silence is one of the great arts of conversation.

(Marcus Tullius Cicero)

I didn't want to investigate the murder of the twins. To immerse in darkness again was a road I had no wish to travel. Battered and wounded by all the loss of previous cases, I had barely managed to survive. Beatings, attacks, had left me with

Mutilated fingers

Hearing problems

A limp

Lethal dreams

And

A shitload of anxiety that Xanax barely kept a lid on. With a new woman in my life and happy for the very first time, would I risk it all?

Nope.

But.

It is that very *but* that has led me astray so many times. A sly curiosity niggled at me so I figured,

"Vague inquiries couldn't hurt."

I had one ally / friend still remaining in the Guards.

Owen Daglish.

He was a drinker of fierce proportions and that might have held my link to him. When I called him, he groaned, said,

"If you want information on *anything,* fuck off now."

I did what you do.

I lied.

Said,

"Hey, I just want to buy you a pint."

We met in the Stage Door. Sounds like a theatrical pub and there is always plenty of drama afoot but, get there early afternoon, it is quiet. Owen was already at the counter, murdering a pint. Seeing me, he said to the barman,

"Couple of large Jamesons."

The barman was a nonnational, asked,

"Ice?"

Like, seriously?

Owen gave him the look, said,

"Not if you want to go on breathing."

Owen was dressed in a cheap suit and cheaper shoes, and his hair needed a trim. He had the look of a guy who had been on the lash for too long. I said,

"You look, um . . . great."

He laughed, said,

"Fuck you."

Got the iceless drinks and moved to a corner table where Owen produced a silver tube and sucked on it.

Vaping.

Blew a cloud of vapor over our heads, said,

"Had to pack in the cigs so I'm reduced to this . . ."

He looked at the tube.

"This shite."

I asked,

"What do know about the twins who were tied together and tossed in the river?"

He sighed deeply, then,

"I thought you were out of this game."

"I am, really, but, you know, sounded like a bizarre case."

He shook his empty glass and I got some refills. I settled for a single Jay. I was meeting Marion later and had to mind my manners. I said,

"*Sláinte.*"

He didn't reciprocate, said,

"Superglue."

"What?"

"Their mouths were sealed with it."

"God almighty."

He took a deep drink, said,

"Takes one sick fuck to do that."

I asked,

"The father, Renaud, what's his story?"

Now he turned to look at me, said,

"You seem awfully interested for a guy who is not investigating."

Time to cough up.

I took out a flat envelope, said,

"A little something for the Garda fund."

He put it quickly in his jacket, then,

"Seriously Jack, stay well away. Renaud was up to his arse in every kind of hedge fund scam. A guy like that, you don't want to be around."

To lighten the mood, I said,

"I appreciate your concern, Owen. It is kind of touching."

He scoffed, said,

"Jack, I couldn't give less of a fuck what happens to you."

On that bright note we parted.

Marion worked as a speech therapist and was offered a chance to attend a conference in America.

Attending a conference in the U.S. was like a mini lottery win in Ireland. Half of the government usually were in on this scam. Plus all the travel expenses to be claimed. She asked,

"Jack, come with me."

Phew.

So many years I had tried to go to America. It was my ultimate dream but always something conspired to ruin the plan. Usually my own self. Life is a bitch. Just when you've deleted the hope it sneaks up and kicks your arse.

I said,

"No."

Cold as that.

She was taken aback and took a few moments to ask,

"Why?"

I said,

"It is not a good time."

She gave a brief, rueful smile, then tried,

"Could you expand a little?"

I always hoped I wouldn't be one of those assholes who whimpered,

"I need you to trust me on this."

I said,

"I need you to trust me on this"

She considered for a moment, then,

"Fuck that."

We had that awkward moment when you basically want to cut and run. The mature thing was to *discuss*.

Thrash out the issue

Ponder a bit

Concede, etc.

I ran.

Joffrey was at the door as I passed and he said,

"Shithead."

Love has no past or future.
So it is with this extraordinary state of silence.

(Jiddu Krishnamurti)

I crawled back to Marion, murmuring contrition. She forgave me in that Irish fashion:

V
   E
     R
       Y

Slowly.

And, of course, with a codicil.

To mind Joffrey.

Like fuck.

I did weakly protest,

"I'm not great with kids."

But she had me by the balls and said,

"I will only be gone a month. Joffrey is staying with relations and *you* . . ."

Pause.

"Could take him out twice a week."

I said,

"I don't think he likes me."

She laughed, said,

"Joffrey doesn't like anybody."

Terrific.

I began a low-key investigation into the deaths of the Renaud twins. It wasn't a mystery as to them being killed but a mystery as to why it hadn't happened sooner.

Like that.

A series of pubs, clubs, and friends all spoke of the sheer nastiness of the boys. Using their money as a weapon, they had abused, bullied, and mocked just about everybody they ever encountered. Three girls at least hinted at rape being part of their repertoire but any allegations had been crushed by the twins' solicitor, named Nery.

I went to see him.

His office was on Merchants Road and consisted of a lot of glass and bespoke granite. I went to reception and a frosty receptionist snapped that I needed an appointment. I decided to test the weight of the family name, said,

"I don't think Mr. Renaud will be very pleased to hear that."

Presto, I was in.

Nery looked like a cricketer gone to seed. Fading blond hair swept in a hopeful quiff, a suit that said,

"Here is serious fucking cash."

He was in his late fifties with a high complexion and eyes that had never alighted on anything they liked. My appearance didn't change that view.

He barked,

"ID?"

I said,

"My name is Jack Taylor and Mr. Renaud hired me to find out what happened to his sons."

Nery grimaced—or it could have been a smile—said,

"They were murdered is what happened."
I said,
"I can hear your deep sorrow even saying that."
His head shot up and he asked,
"Sarcasm? Well, some washed-up drunk comes into my office and gives me . . . sarcasm?"
I wanted to slap his well-fed face but went with,
"Any light you could shed on the matter?"
He sniggered, said,
"Thomas is going to get a kick out of this."
"Thomas?"
"Thomas Clancy, superintendent of the Guards."
I held my hand up, said,
"Lemme guess. A golf crony?"
He picked up some papers, said,
"Good day, sir."
I didn't move.
He looked up, said,
"You're dismissed."
I turned to leave, left with,
"Funny, that's the exact same thing the Guards said to me."

It is said that if you are at the Claddagh Basin in the hour before dawn, after Saint Brigid's Day, and you sit very still, you can see the famine ships glide across the bay and along the wind hear the faint whisper of the names of the coffin ships.

Emma Prescott
Joshua Carroll
Margaret Milne
C. H. Appleton
The Luculus
William Kerry

So it was that I was thus perched, at the end of that bitter cold month, looking at Nimmo's Pier. Not so long ago, I had stood on that very spot, a revolver in my hand and suicide on my breath. To this day, I'm not sure what turned me 'round.

I saw a man there now, standing real close to the edge, almost exactly the place I had stood. Shook my head to dispel the illusion.

He jumped.

I muttered,

"Fuck."

I tore off my Garda all-weather coat, shucked my shoes, and went in the water.

Christ, it was cold. I lost sight of him twice and he was going down for the final time when I reached him. I grabbed his collar with my hand and kicked for shore. He fought me, the bad bastard. Nearly drowned us until I got a fist to his chin and stunned him.

Pulled him up the shore and collapsed. He was muttering, "Cold, so cold."

I got to my feet and retrieved my coat, wrapped him in it, then got my phone and called an ambulance. My whole body shook. I reached back into my jacket, got the flask, got some of the Jay into the man's mouth. Took a long swig my own self.

The ambulance came within minutes with a squad car right behind. I explained the situation. The attendants got the man wrapped fast and offered me a blanket, said,

"You better come too."

I said no.

I saw the flash of an iPhone. Damn dog walker.

The Guards treated me with suspicion. One of them suddenly said,

"God almighty, it's Taylor."

His partner, young and eager, asked,

"Who's that?"

The older guy said,

"Trouble is what he is."

Leveled a hard stare at me, barked,

"What are you doing here, this time of the morning?"

The ambulance attendant said,

"Being a hero, is what."

I took a slug from the flask to the disapproval of both Guards.

The ambulance attendant handed me my coat, said,

"You might well have saved that man from hypothermia."

Not to mention drowning but I said nothing.

The young Guard grabbed the coat, said,
"That is an official Garda coat. I'll write you up for that."
The attendant said,
"Christ, don't be a bollix."
My thoughts exactly but they kept the coat.
Before the ambulance departed, I went over to check on the man. He managed to sit up and beckoned me. I was ready to say,
"No need to thank me."
He leaned real close, whispered,
"Fuck you."
The ambulance guy heard him and, as he prepared to leave, said,
"It's the shock."
I thought about that, answered,
"He's probably a Guard."
Coatless, I made my wet, frozen way home.

26

We need silence to be able to touch souls.

(Mother Teresa)

The country was reeling under a double horror.

The Grace case where vulnerable children were left in a home where abuse of all kinds was not only *known* to have occurred but had been reported numerous times to the department of health. Grace was removed once, but

Then returned to the same home.

And this was not a matter of months but twenty years.

As people tried to find some way of analyzing this, it was revealed that a

Septic tank, yes a *septic tank,* was the dumping place for babies of unwed mothers or mothers *deemed unfit,* and children up to three years old had been thus dumped. A cursory search had disclosed that at least eighty-five bodies were

Thrown there.

The order of nuns in charge of the poor women refused to take any responsibility and had indeed hired a PR lady who, on hearing of the accusations, replied,

"So?"

Further, she told a TV crew investigating that the most they would find was

"A few old bones."

I made the papers.

"Local hero saves drowning man."

They detailed how ex-Garda John . . .

John!

" . . . Taylor risked his life to save a man in the Claddagh Basin."

It didn't mention the Guards confiscating my beloved coat.

In the pub, I took a fair amount of slagging.

Like

"*Oh, save me Johnny.*"

"*Throw us a lifeline, John boy.*"

It did earn me some free drinks. I was on my second of these when Renaud appeared. Not, alas, to praise me.

Opened with,

"You have time to jump in rivers when you should be searching for the killer of my sons?"

I nearly said,

"I was looking for clues."

But went with,

"I found nothing in my investigation."

He looked like he might spit in my drink.

Which would have been a very, *very* bad idea.

I finished my drink, brushed past him out to the street. He followed me, uttering a string of French invectives. He reminded me of somebody.

On a wall opposite was a tag that was to be found all over the city.

2

4

J

I was staring at it when Renaud grabbed my arm, shouted,
"You are fired."
I turned to him, the penny dropping. I said,
"Trump! You are the spit of the Donald."
He laughed almost manically, exclaimed,
"*Le Donald, c'est magnifique.*"

The true genius shudders at incompleteness and usually prefers silence to saying something which is not everything it should be.

(Edgar Allan Poe)

The Tuam babies scandal rocked Irish life to its core.

How do you even vaguely understand how nuns . . .

Nuns!

Dumped the bodies of babies and very young children into a septic tank.

The Grace shock.

A vulnerable girl, later as an adult, was left for twenty years with foster parents who abused her in every way there is.

And

Despite social workers' reports, even after she was temporarily removed, was then put back into the same viper's hole. And other children and adults too.

All vulnerable and horrendously molested.

You listened to the news, the reports and, truly, your jaw dropped.

Enda Kenny, our much-maligned leader of the coalition government, responded with one of the finest speeches of barely contained rage.

Said,

> "We did not just hide away the dead bodies
> Of tiny human beings.
> We dug deeper
> To bury

Our compassion,

Our mercy

And

Our very humanity."

Amid all this horror, you strove desperately to find a reason even to stir from bed. Got some through football.

For once, the beautiful game was . . . beautiful.

Barcelona were four down going into the second match with Paris Saint-Germain. The papers had crucified Barca in the week leading up to the second match.

Incredulous, I read descriptions of

Has been

Finished.

I mean, seriously?

You can never, ever write off such a team. I knew that team would roar back with absolute ferocity.

Did they just.

Not only had they to score four but, when PSG scored, they had to up the ante again.

And again.

And, fuck me,

Again.

Never have I seen such a comeback.

I'm not your up-on-his-feet shouting at matches unless it's Galway in the hurling and even then I'm relatively mild.

I was up
Shouting
Wild.
And only sorry I hadn't my beloved pup to dance with.

Thinking of dogs, my heart was scalded by the memory of my gorgeous dog.

Storm.

And a tiny hurricane he was.

Jesus.

I wept when they killed him.

And in such a vicious bloody fashion.

The maniac who did it had a warped awful sense of twisted humor.

Cut the pup's heart out

And

Left this note, with the heart literally in the middle of the sentence:

I *heart* Fenians.

I made an unholy pact to enter the darkness of my own mind. The cold place where nothing lives.

I did so with vengeance aforethought.

Did I fucking ever.

And knew such a price as would ensue from that dark territory. They mutter,

"For revenge, then dig two graves."

I dug a whole brutal field.
I was not consoled.
I would never again go *gentle* into any sane night.
Ever.
I knew and I was content.

Back Rank Checkmates

In chess, a rank is a row of squares across the board.
Your back rank is the row where you place your king.
Be very careful. Many checkmates are delivered
On the back of the board.

(*Beginning Chess*)

I was listening to Jimmy Norman's show. He plays the best music for rock heads. News on top of the hour revealed that

1,487

Bodies of children were now believed to be in the septic tank in Tuam.

1,487. Jesus indeed wept.

The nuns named in the allegations, Bon Secours, whose very name implied

Help and succor, were hiding behind a PR lady who told a newspaper,

"You'll find nothing in the tank but old bones from *the famine.*"

She had since remained incommunicado.

The night before, reeling from Irish horrors, a search-and-rescue helicopter rushing to the aid of a Russian seaman was lost off the Mayo coast, with all four crew missing.

Desperate for mind distraction,

I binged on

Suburra

Spotless

Gomorrah.

Then found a small gem of a Western,

Bone Tomahawk.

With Kurt Russell and Patrick Wilson.

I made a double espresso, black, bitter like the very air of the present, heard

Marc Roberts on his show give a shout-out to Johnny Duhan's *Winter.*

The doorbell chimed and I swore, muttered,

"Better be bloody good."

Opened it to a stranger.

A man in a very fine long suede jacket, dark cords, and what seemed to be white

Converse. He was tall, in that vague fiftyish bracket, buzz-cut black hair, a hawk nose, and eyes that the romantic novelists might call burning.

He had that Russell Crowe gig of quiet smoldering going on. I snapped,

"Yeah?"

He put out his hand, a rough callused one, said,

"They call me Tevis."

I had no clue, said,

"I have no clue."

He gave a wide grin, the kind of shit-eating one that Trump would like, said,

"You saved my life. From drowning."

I wittily said,

"Oh."

He asked,

"Might I come in?"

Why not.

He took a brief scan of the living room, checked the panorama of the bay, said,

"Fantastic view."

I offered,

"Something to drink?"

He seemed to like that, said,

"I could go a stiff one."

Somehow, in that Brit fashion, investing it with a vague lewdness. Caught that his own self, added,

"I'm a bit nervous. I mean, how often do you get to thank your savior?"

I detected a hint of sarcasm, so went with,

"If you're Catholic, just about every day, they recommend."

He smiled, great capped teeth, no National Health dance there. He said,

"They told me you were a hoot."

"They?"

"Don't be coy, Jack. May I call you Jack? The dogs in the street tell tales about you, man! You're a goddamn genuine legend,"

Suddenly, I was tired.

He smiled, asked,

"Where are we on that drink?"

I said,

"Bar's closed. It's Good Friday."

He did a mock emo face, then put his hand in his jacket. I shot out, grabbed his wrist, said,

"You best just have attitude in there."

Raised his eyebrows, said,

"Bit jumpy, fella, maybe cut back on the caffeine."

Then handed me a small marble figurine.

"As my thanks to you, Jack, I am going to teach you some first-rate chess."

The figure was heavy in my hand and beautifully carved, I said,

"It's a knight."

He gave a short hand clap, said,

"See? You're learning already."

When I finally persuaded him that he had to *actually* leave, he said,

"A man of books like your good self will know what the Chinese say."

I sighed, sounding horrendously like my mother, who could have sighed for Ireland and did,

Often.

I asked,

"Do tell?"

"You save a man's life, you are thus responsible for that life."

"Like fuck,"

I answered.

He headed for the door, said,

"You and me, buddy, now we are joined at the hip."

I watched him from the bay window. He stood on the promenade, gazing at the water. I could hope he might be reassessing that body of water for another go.

He turned, gave what can only be described as a *cheery wave.*

I poured a large Jay, the bishop lined up alongside. The glass hit against it, knocked it to the ground. I bent, picked it up, noticed letters on the base.

Peered close, read,

2

4

J

The
Chessman
Cometh

Peter Boyne was a pedophile

And

Proud.

No fake remorse, no contrite wailing.

He had been a priest for years but even the Church couldn't cover for him and booted him. He even looked like the notorious Brendan Smith. Soft build, weak face, and bulging eyes.

"I'm an ugly cunt,"

He told a victim.

But never charged.

Never.

The luck of the very wicked devil.

He gazed at the mound of trophies on his bed.

Red baby socks.

A small Lakers T-shirt.

Tiny hurdle.

Barney the dinosaur.

Teletubbies; he could name them all.

Laa-Laa, Dipsy, and had a way to incorporate then into a song, right before he used the chloroform.

And photos.

Hundreds.

He swooned with the joy of vivid remembrance.

Now.

He had his sights fixed on a new boy.

He'd learned his name, of course, and toned that with an orgasmic slowness:

J-o-f-f-r-e-y.

I don't know what love is.

I hated my mother so not a great beginning.

I cared for my little dog as if my life depended on it and in a bizarre way it did.

I think I loved my dead friends.

Ridge,

Stewart.

But I certainly never showed it to them.

Not so they'd notice.

And a woman named Ann Henderson; I was truly obsessed with her. She did the big thing and, in Galway, by that we mean

Suicide.

Not a great record then.

Along came Marion.

Phew-oh.

She looked like Kate Mara, whose part in *House of Cards* was compelling. She was the sister of the more glamorous, successful Romola Garai. In common with the actress, Marion combined that blend of sheer spirit with vulnerability.

I'm a sucker for that shit.

Let me digress as a Booker novelist might do.

Eamon Casey, our former bishop, died.

In the same time frame as

Chuck Berry

Jimmy Breslin

Martin McGuinness. (Norman Tebbit said he hoped McGuinness would rot in hell for all eternity, adding he was a coward.)

Nice.

Eamon had been our most popular cleric, and if the Church ever seemed to be part of the people it was due to the likes of him.

Until,

Like the fallible human being he was, he fell in love.

No harm there.

But

He covered it up—and the birth of a child.

Until

The dame went on *The Late Late Show* and blew him out of the ecclesial water.

He resigned, despite the pope asking him not to.

He went into exile in South America and eventually came home to live a life of quiet desperation. Much like De Niro's priest in *True Confessions*.

Marion went to his funeral and, in a bizarre move, the Church that had effectively banished him declared he would be buried in the crypt under Galway Cathedral.

Marion attended the funeral Mass in the cathedral. It was officiated by the archbishop. Eamon Casey had stood up to gun-wielding thugs when Archbishop Romero was assassinated.

As a young priest in London he had performed Trojan work among the poor.

So

What did the arch say in his speech on Eamon?

You guessed it.

Focused only on the *sin*.

Yup, lambasted the poor man, and spoke about how he had humiliated the people closest to him.

No fragging mention of the Church's own record on child abuse.

Marion was spitting iron. Very nearly stood up and shouted at the arch.

Not doing so was one of the great regrets of her life.

So she wrote to him.

Like this:

"Dear Reverence / Irreverence,

I have been a regular attendant at Mass all my life.

I raised my son Catholic.

I pay my tithes.

I do the Nine Friday novenas.

I went to the funeral Mass of our beloved Bishop Eamon Casey.

You may have disbarred him but he will always be *Our Bishop*.

I was not expecting you to actually *praise* the man.

God forbid the Church would ever demonstrate such grace.

But

to castigate him,
Literally denounce him
All over again,
To the exclusion of the other shining deeds of his life, before his assembled family.
How dare you.
In our cathedral?
Yes, our money, alms, built it.
Shame on you.
The young people of Ireland don't even know who you are. But to us who do, you owed at the very least a tiny hint of balance.
I know you won't have the grit to answer me unless some lackey sends me the standard corn.
. . . *your comments have been noted etc.*
I expect you will do what the Church has excelled in:
Nothing.
God mind you better than you minded your brave bishop.
Yours in disappointment,
Marion R. Coyle."
The Church did as she predicted.
Nothing.

Hotel
on
the corner
of
Bitter
and
Sweet.

The first outing I took Joffrey on left a lot to be desired.

I tried not to stare at his Little Lord Fauntleroy outfit.

I mean, fuck, really?

White pants, navy blue shirt, and, I kid thee not, a knitted wool tie, with a blazer, complete with crest.

I was wearing battered 501s, scuffed Doc Martens, my way beat-up leather jacket. I was determined to try and bond with this little gobshite, but seriously?

I said,

"We're not planning on the opera, are we?"

He sneered, turned his mean little mouth down.

"I doubt you'd be too familiar with that scenario."

Scenario.

I was determined to be upbeat, began,

"Thought we'd swing by Supermac's, grab us some bad boy burgers."

He stopped, literally in his tracks, asked,

"You are serious?"

Okay, now we were cruising.

I said with gusto,

"Oh, yeah, and you can add curried chips if the fancy takes you."

He said with venom,

"I don't do carbs."

Oh.

I hung on to the fading gusto, asked,

"What would you like? Italian, Cajun?"

He seemed to actually focus. Then,

"They have any sushi bars in this burg?"

His accent was a horror blend of clipped Brit with sprinkled American. I echoed,

"Raw fish? You want raw fish?"

I'll admit my energy was flagging but, fuck, I persisted.

Said,

"Kid like you, you need to get some spuds, bacon, and cabbage in you."

He put two fingers to his mouth, made the gagging sound.

I sighed, said,

"I'll take that as a no."

He began to stare at his phone, as the whole nation currently does.

I'd have sold his miserable hide for one shot of Jameson.

I said,

"We can swing by my flat, I'll rustle up something and, hey . . ."

My voice had risen in nigh panic.

"I have some games there."

He lit up, asked,

"You're a gamer?"

Modesty be damned, I said,

"It has been suggested in the not so recent past that I do indeed *have game.*"

He gave me a blank look, which did not add to his overall charm, shook his head as if it clear it of nonsense, asked,

"Whatcha got? Like Assassins Creed, Warcraft Three, Mafiosi Four?"

I was lost, tried,

"I've got Monopoly and, well, that's it."

He mimicked spitting, said,

"Board games." (His voice rising on the end bit.) "You can't be serious, I mean it's so . . ."

Searched for a word to convey utter contempt, got

"Retro."

Sharp as a whip, I snapped,

"Retro is the new cool. Get with, dare I say, *the game?*"

While this brisk exchange batted back and forth, an over-weight guy in a T-shirt with the logo

SIN AN SCEAL (That's the story)

actually drooled as he eyed Joffrey. His hands in his dirty sweat-pants, he actually groaned, muttered,

"Soon my love."

You'd know the very last thing to do with the child of the woman in your life is to bring him to a pub.

Right.

I know that.

Brought him to the pub.

Sat him at a table in the back, him going,

"Mother won't be pleased."

Gee, you think?

I didn't ask him what he wanted. I was all through with that gig. The bar guy peered over at him, asked,

"Your boy?"

Like fuck.

I said,

"Whatever else, mine he isn't."

A wag along the bar said,

"The clergy got in trouble for that kind of thing."

I gave him the look.

Asked the bar guy for

Double Jay,

Pint back,

Bag of whatever flavor crisps,

Large Coke.

Guy asked,

"He want ice in that?"

"Shovel it in."

I sank the Jay there and then, tasted like vague hope. Over to the kid with my goodies, said,

"Here you go."

He pushed the Coke aside, said,

"That is equal to nine full spoons of sugar."

I wanted so badly to wallop him.

I asked,

"And your point is?"

He sighed as in . . . *Lord grant me patience with fools.*

Said,

"My mother didn't pay top dollar for dental work for some nincompoop to force pure sugar down my throat."

Force?

Nincompoop?

The kid was like an escapee from a poor-rate Evelyn Waugh. In desperation I reached in my pocket and found the chess piece that Tevis gave me.

Joffrey's eyes lit up, asked,

"A chess piece?"

I put it on the table and he picked it up, examined the writing on the base, the

2

4

J

I said,

"I dunno what that means."

He scoffed, said,

"It's obvious."

Fuck.

Okay. Asked,

"What?"

"Two for Justice."

I mulled that over, figuring, Some form of vigilante? Next time I saw Tevis, we'd have us a chat.

So I tried to cut some slack for the kid, asked,

"What would you like to drink?"

"Still water with a slice of lemon. Ballygowan or Evian at a pinch."

I went to the counter, said to the bar guy,

"Glass of tap water, shove some lemon in it."

He seemed puzzled, said,

"We have all the top brands."

I stared at him, asked,

"You hard of hearing?"

Got what was not the cleanest glass and very wilted lemon, which, to no great surprise, the kid pushed aside, said,

"I called my mother."

Oh, fuck.

I whined,

"Oh, no, c'mon."

He smiled with devilish glee, said,

"You're for the high jump."

I leaned right into him, snarled,

"What is your fucking problem, son?"

He pulled back, said,

"I don't like you."

I smiled, threatened,

"Get used to it, punk. I'm here for the long haul."

He stood up, said,

"I very much doubt that, mister."

As I followed him out, I asked,

"Apart from the water, do you think it went pretty good otherwise?"

I followed him as he walked at a brisk pace toward the square. I wondered what he'd pull next.

A taxi.

I kid thee not. And he turned as he got in, gave me the finger.

I watched the cab head toward the docks.

Hate to admit it but I had a sort of sneaking admiration for the little bastard.

Removing the Defender

There are ways of removing your opponent's
defending pieces that leave others open to attack.

(Beginning Chess)

A second helicopter was lost.

Unbelievable.

Based in the UK, it contained a family flying to Ireland for a confirmation.

Unlike those from the first helicopter, the bodies were recovered quickly.

R 117, the search-and-rescue helicopter, still had two of the crew missing despite a massive search.

To see the families waiting reminded me of the widows in the Claddagh back in the harsh days as they awaited news of their husbands and sons.

Ochre ochon (woe is me indeed).

I was in my apartment, staring out at the bay and thinking how much the very ocean played such a part in our collective history.

The doorbell rang, a quiet ring as if the caller hoped I wasn't home. I opened the door to Tevis, the man whose life I saved and who was now becoming a fucking nuisance. He offered a bottle, said,

"Old Kentucky sipping bourbon."

And,

"Six genuine longnecks. If you read your crime fiction as much as you pretend to, you'll know it's the preferred tipple of Craig McDonald."

I said,

"That is one long sentence."

He laughed, moved past me, said,

"Like life."

I followed him in, put the beers in the fridge, and turned to him. He pulled out a pack of unfiltered Camels, said,

"Eddie Bunker's favorite."

I asked,

"You came to educate me on the tastes of crime writers?"

He stood before the bay window, asked,

"Like glasses?"

Marion had given me a set of Galway crystal to spruce up the apartment, said,

"Taylor, you need some style."

She used my surname when she was being playful. *Jack* when I was in deep shit. Alas, she was using my Christian name a lot more frequently. I took out two of those heavy babes, poured the bourbon, admired the way the light caught the glass, like a tiny whispered prayer.

Truth is, though, I'd have drunk out of a wellington if my need was great.

He said,

"Nice glasses."

"My mother's,"

I lied.

He said,

"Ah, Irish lads and the mammie."

As fucking if.

He knocked back the drink in jig time. I went,

"Whoa, like what happened to the *sipping* bit?"

He gave me what he probably figured was a roguish smile, said,

"Partner, we're a long ways from Kentucky."

I took a sip, asked,

"What do you want?"

He did the mock-offended gig, said,

"You don't like me."

True.

I said,

"True."

He asked,

"Is it because I'm gay?"

I said,

"I didn't know that. I don't care if you like sheep."

A silence.

Then he asked,

"Sheep?"

Enough with the sipping, I walloped back the drink, gasped, muttered,

"Phew-oh."

Gathered my thoughts somewhat, tried,

"What's the deal with the chess piece and the message on the base, the

Two for Justice?"

He applauded, literally, said,

"Well done, you figured it out, smarter than you act, methinks."

His accent was now channeling Barry Fitzgerald via Dublin 4. Not an appealing tone. He put down his glass, said,

"Fill her up and I'll fill you in."

Managed to insert a certain mild menace into the sound.

I poured us both fresh ones, waited.

He launched.

"I had a decent living as an accountant. I work out, as is evident."

Here, he flexed his upper body, did a small pirouette, continued,

"At the gym, as you do, I met my lover, a rather splendid fellow."

Now he was aping Cumberbatch.

"We settled into a jolly old existence until . . ."

His face darkened.

"Until the twins, the Renaud twins, decided to engage in a little light gay bashing."

He looked at me, asked,

"You know what the brain looks like after repeated kicks?"

How the fuck would I know that?

I stayed in low gear, shook my head.

He said,

"Like mushy peas."

He shook a cig out of the Camel pack, so expertly that it had to have been rehearsed. Never no mind, it's impressive.

He continued but now in a flat monotone.

"So, when a man contacted me, asked if I wanted justice, I said, You betcha."

I poured us more sipping well-being, delaying any comment until I could get my head 'round this, then asked,

"You killed no twins?"

"No, of course not."

"Who did?"

He drew out a tense silence, said,

"Pierre Renaud, their dad."

"Are you frightened?" she asked.

"I haven't peed my pants yet," I said, "but then, it's been a while between beers."

"He might just do," the fella said. "He's got that 'born to lose and lose violently' about him."

Pause.

"That's good."

(Daniel Woodrell, *Tomato Red*)

I tried to take in what Tevis had said, asked,

"You're claiming the twins' own father killed his sons?"

He let out a tolerant sigh, said,

"I'm not claiming anything, I'm telling you what happened."

Fuck.

I said,

"God almighty, to murder his family."

He corrected me,

"Just two of them."

I poured a drink but it didn't seem to be having much effect. Maybe the sipping wasn't really my style. I asked,

"Did he say why?"

He shook his head, said,

"I didn't ask."

Fuck that.

I demanded,

"Come on, seriously?"

He lit another Camel, said,

"I was in a blizzard of grief, rage, madness. I would have paid for revenge."

That I grasped, having recently visited such territory my own self. I said,

"I'm trying to picture him actually doing that."

Tevis said,

"He didn't."

I wanted to fling him across the room, shouted,

"You're changing the story?"

He stood up, tired of the narrative, said,

"He had help."

"Someone else?"

He shrugged, said,

"You hardly think a father would drown his own sons? I mean, get with the program, buddy."

Enough.

I was across the room, grabbed him by the shirt collar, pushed him fast and hard against the wall, snarled,

"*Stop* fucking with me and answer the question without any more mind-fucking, got it?"

I was so enraged I could have beaten him to a pulp. I wanted it so badly I could taste metal in my mouth.

He nodded and I let him go.

Pulled himself together, tried to light a cig but tremors in his hands betrayed him. Instead, he gulped his booze, then,

"There is a man, served three tours in Iraq and had the distinction of surviving three bomb attacks. He understandably developed a phobia about noise. He now specializes in what the Americans term *wet work*. More prosaically, he kills people. They call him the *Silence*."

I asked,

"And you met him?"

"Only once, and it was enough. He is the most nondescript man you'd ever see or, as the case may be, *not see*. He looks like every bad photo fit. He doesn't turn up at the time you'd arranged and, just as you give up, prepare to leave, he is standing behind you."

I was intrigued, tried to keep my tone skeptical, asked,

"What did he say to you?"

Tevis looked around as if he expected the man to be behind him, then,

"He asked me if I knew the value of silence."

My mind was alight with so much craziness. I asked,

"And this mystery man, how does one find him?"

Tevis smiled, a hint of smugness there, said,

"You place a chess quote in the *Irish Times*."

Then he gave a soft tap to his head, exclaimed,

"Oh my gawd, how could I forget?"

And ran to the door.

Then back a moment later, carrying a large parcel, said,

"As a wee token of my deep gratitude."

Suspicious, I pulled the paper off to reveal my all-weather Garda coat, and like new!

He said,

"I took the liberty of having it dry-cleaned and, trust me fella, an expensive job."

Not sure what to say, I asked,

"How did you? I mean . . ."

He shrugged, said,

"I made the young Guard who took it an offer he couldn't refuse."

I was impressed, I think, said,

"Thank you."

He made a dismissive wave, said,

"You saved my life, I saved your coat. Seems fair."

I pushed then.

"You felt guilty about those twins, and that's why you were going in the water?"

He gave me a long look.

"Fuck no. I was depressed about my lover. But the twins? I was delighted they got theirs."

Pawn Carnage

One rook on the seventh rank is an advantage
but two are usually unstoppable.

(Beginning Chess)

Jimmy Reagan was a close friend of my father. They went to the dogs together. Greyhound racing, in College Road. Were the races fixed?

Let me say this.

One evening as my dad headed into the track, a man stopped him, asked for his race card, and then marked every single race. Said,

"We mind our own."

All six dogs won.

After my dad died, Jimmy really went to the dogs.

The *demon* drink was mentioned.

I met him a few years back. He stood in a doorway, wearing what was once a very fine suit. I gave him a few quid. He said,

"Jackie boy, see this suit? I bought it from the winnings me and yer dad had."

His face got a wistful look and he added,

"Ah, sweet Lord, that was the best night of me lousy life."

Such men were not built for rehabs. They slipped through the cracks of society, like sad ghosts of what might have been.

He was found dead in an alley, wearing the suit. I was told he had no one to bury him so I took care of it. Brought the one suit to the dry cleaner. The guy there said,

"In its day, this was really something."

I said,

"Weren't we all?"

He asked,

"Going somewhere special?"

"The cemetery."

Odd, he didn't ask me anything after that.

The funeral was bare, like the poor bastard's life. Me, the priest, and two gravediggers. It rained.

I phoned Pierre Renaud but he was unavailable. I even went to his home but the house looked dead, like his sons, I guess. I wasn't sure what exactly to do about him. Crossed my mind to set the Silence on him. How poetic would that be? If I did find him, how to begin?

"Did you have your sons killed?"

There's a showstopper.

Tell the Guards?

Oh, yeah, like they had such a high opinion of me to begin with.

But

I could tell one Guard.

Arranged to meet Owen Daglish. He was not happy, asked,

"What do you want now?"

Not encouraging.

I said,

"In fact, I might have some information that would further your career."

"Yeah, that will be the day."

We met in Garavan's. He yet again looked the very worst for wear, said,

"I can't talk until I get behind two drinks."

So we did that.

The change was near miraculous. Years seemed to drop from his face, his eyes opened, and his whole physical stature improved. He grinned, said,

"That is the biz."

Looked at me, asked,

"How is that new lady of yours?"

"In America."

He seemed to think about that, then,

"Will she come back?"

I acted like I was offended, which I was a little, asked,

"Why wouldn't she?"

He gave a low whistle, said,

"Because you're Jack!"

Not really an area I wished to pursue so I laid out the whole story of the guy named Silence and the murder of the twins.

He asked,

"The father had his sons killed?"

I nodded.

He took a long swig of his drink, then,

"That is bollocks."

I pushed.

"But what if it's not?"

He took a long hard look at me, said,

"Whatever it is, you need to leave it alone. The Guards think you're the worst kind of trouble. If you tell them one of the town's alumni is a killer, a guy who golfs with the superintendent, I mean, they're going to kick your arse."

I went to protest but he said,

"Leave it alone, Jack, and leave me alone."

He stood up, a look of resignation on his face. I asked,

"Don't you want another drink?"

He said,

"Oh, yeah, just not with you."

The BBC showed the fourth and final series of *Luther*, starring Idris Elba. Luther is living in a house that is on the edge of a cliff and daily sliding toward doom. A cop asks him how he is.

"Tickety boo," he answered.

"Totally disco."

I was sitting in Eyre Square, on a bench close to the garden plaque for JFK.

As a child, I'd sat on my father's shoulders watching the presidential car

Go by.

We sure loved JFK.

Not a whole lot of heroes since.

The Guards were in a whole load of shite. It was alleged they had tried to smear and destroy the career of a noted whistle-blower. Now, it seemed that over half a million breath tests had the figures inflated. The Garda commissioner refused to explain or resign.

Theresa May in the UK called a snap election.

I wondered how I got out of bed and, indeed, how the commissioner got out.

Trump was trying to cut the income tax rate for multinationals by fifteen percent to lure companies back to America.

I was watching the Meyrick Hotel when a slew of black SUVs pulled up.

Rock stars, I wondered?

Out hopped Father Malachy.

A longtime enemy, he had been my mother's lapdog back in the days when vitreous women had a tame priest in tow to demonstrate their piety. Noting my mother was one cold bitch, you can guess what her priest was like.

Time back, I came into possession of *The Red Book*, a book of heresy that the Church was anxious to suppress. Bad publicity was the last thing it wanted.

Malachy inveigled me into parting with the book.

He had instantly become the Church darling. Of course, any attempts to reach him after were shunned. I headed for the hotel. The doorman was about to block me when he recognized me, said,

"Howyah, Jack?"

I asked,

"What's the occasion?"

He raised his eyes to heaven, said,

"The Rotary Club are honoring some priest."

Some priest indeed.

I spotted Malachy in the midst of a group of people. Least, I thought it was him but changed—changed utterly. A stunning new black suit, tiny hint of purple at the neck collar. I'd seen that on trainee bishops.

Bishop?

Surely not.

But then, in a Trump world, who knew? His hair was what I can only call *coiffed*. I'm not entirely sure what that means save that it's not on the card of any barber I ever frequented.

More, he wasn't smoking.

Him, the ultimate diehard nicotine fiend. I approached and two young priests with, I swear, earpieces like sub–special agents blocked my path. Malachy saw me, said,

"Allow."

Imperious.

I asked,

"What the fuck happened?"

One of the young priests pushed me, warned,

"Watch the tone."

Malachy smiled, benevolently, as in *suffer the little children.* He said,

"My dear, wild, uncouth Jack."

What the hell was he taking?

He sounded *benign.*

I knew then that even his name was indeed Malachi, no more Malachy.

He said,

"I have been the unworthy recipient of many blessings."

I was near speechless. I tried,

"*The Red Book*, it made you a star."

He smiled, touch of the old Malachy seeping through, though the yellow teeth of yore were now glorious white. He said,

"We are aware of your own tiny contribution to the miracle."

Tiny.

I asked,

"Do you actually believe your own bullshit?"

Got another dig from one of the minders. Malachi said,

"We'll try and fit you in, to have afternoon tea at the Residence."

He raised his hand in blessing and, I swear, if he patted my head I'd have taken his blessed arm from the elbow. A hint of the old priest peered through the smoke screen and he withdrew his hand. He intoned,

"God mind you well, my son."

And he was gone.

I headed out, the door guy waited, his eyes dancing with curiosity. He asked,

"How'd it go?"

I gave the answer that offered me the only chance to use the expression. I said,

"Totally disco."

A young man, four times with his license suspended, got behind the wheel of a Toyota Corolla. He had been on a marathon drinking session, downing fourteen pints of lager, followed by three shots of tequila. The now standard kill rate for young motorists. At over 100 mph, he plowed into a Mini Cooper, killing a young mother and her daughter.

His defense cited his depression and deep remorse. *His* life, said the defense, was ruined.

Yeah.

He got eighteen months suspended and a year's probation.
He celebrated in the nearest pub.
He wouldn't, he said,
"Drink tequila anymore."
A week later, in a field near a bus stop, he was found with his suspended license shoved down his throat, the word *silence* written in red marker across his forehead.

I got a call from Marion.
It did not begin well. She started,
"What were you thinking?"
Now when Jay Leno asked that of Hugh Grant after the Los Angeles hooker scandal, his tone was friendly, perplexed, as in
"Hey buddy, we get it, kind of."
Marion's tone was
Ice
    To
        Coldest
Felt.
She did not *get it.*
I tried for bumbling but lovable rogue, said,
"I thought the kid might be thirsty."
She echoed,
"*The kid.*"
"Sorry, Joff."

Fucked up again as she *ice* corrected,

"Joffrey."

Phew.

Then,

"You think a *pub* . . ."

Let the word hover like a goddamn virus until,

"Is suitable for *my* child?"

I wanted to say,

"Actually, the docks would be the best place for the brat."

But for once in my fucked-up life I went with caution, tried,

"I'll do better next time."

Silence.

Then,

"There won't be a next time. He said you tried to get him to smoke."

"What?"

I could actually sense the sheer rage coming over the phone. She said,

"Joffrey said that you said every boy needs to break loose."

I was nearly speechless.

Nearly.

Said,

"He is a liar."

Phew-oh.

She let the loaded word swim a bit, then,

"You are calling my son, *my son,* a liar?"

"I am."

She hung up.

Save for the wee touch of trouble at the end, I think it went fairly okay otherwise.

Silence encourages the tormentor,
never the tormented.

(Elie Wiesel)

I was in the pub, the guy beside me saying,

"Listen to this."

I said,

"Sure."

Block out the click of Marion hanging up. The guy said,

"The White House has fallen into the hands of a bully, a boor, and a braggart, a demagogue who taunts his neighbors and revels in his own ignorance."

He looked at me, checking I was paying attention. I made a vague sound of assent.

He continued.

"To his supporters he is a hero who speaks for the white working class against the sneering East Coast elite."

He drained his glass, making a small burping sound, then called for a refill, got it, and asked me,

"You're thinking Trump, right?"

Nope.

I was thinking,

"Shut the fuck up."

He pounced.

"That was Andrew Jackson in, get this, 1829."

Okay, I was a little interested, said,

"Wow."

He wasn't quite done with the quiz aspect, asked,

"You ever see a snap of the man?"

Andrew Jackson?

I said,

"Not so I recall."

He was delighted, said,

"You've seen a twenty-dollar bill?"

"Well, yeah, probably."

"Then you've seen Jackson."

He looked 'round as if the whole pub might have been mesmerized.

They weren't.

But he wasn't about to give it up, pulled a page of a newspaper from his jacket, shoved it in my face, asked,

"What do you see?"

For a brief moment, I could see this lonely bastard in his lonely room, scouring the papers for articles that might make him appear interesting. That deeply saddened me so I looked at the cutting, saw a guy in what seemed to be very dirty stained jeans. I said,

"He's got soiled jeans."

He was near frothing now, said,

"Guess what he paid for them?"

I gave one last try, said,

"Don't know."

With glee, he said,

"Four hundred fifty quid. It's the new fashion."

I asked the obvious,

"Why?"

The drink turned on him, turned him mean as a snake. He snarled,

"Why? What the fuck do you mean *why*? It shows the world has gone apeshit."

I asked with exaggerated patience,

"You're only realizing that now?"

He took a step back, the brawler preparing to launch, mouthed,

"You think you're better than me?"

I asked,

"The old Irish green pound note, who was on it?"

It confused him, he spluttered,

"What?"

"Yeah, the green note, back when the country was still Irish."

He was showing tiny bits of foam on his mouth, spat,

"Who the fuck knows that?"

I said in a very patient, almost Dr. Phil tone,

"That's the trouble with this country. We know who is on the dollar bill but not our own history."

He tried to weigh the weight of the insult, decided to go with,

"Hey, I'm an Irishman."

I shook my head, said,

"What you are is a buffoon."

Now he began his swing but his hand was grabbed from behind, moved up fast behind his back. A familiar voice said,

"Now you don't want to be a nuisance."

Tevis.

Who then bum-marched the guy outside, all in the space of a few seconds.

Came back in, said,

"He decided to call it a day."

I was impressed, said,

"Fancy footwork."

He signaled to the bar guy for a round, said,

"Ballroom dancing, always a help."

I asked,

"Are you following me?"

His pint was in his hand and he held up the glass to the light. The Guinness appeared to shine, if such a thing were possible. I had found that many things were possible with drink, if only briefly. He said,

"Such dark beauty."

He drained half in an impressive gulp, said,

"But nothing lasts and, yes, I was indeed following you."

"Why?"

He motioned to a table and we moved there. He settled himself, then,

"The man they call Silence goes by the name of Allen. He asked me to tell you he is about to do you a major favor."

I was in no mood for mind-fucking, leaned close, snarled,

"I don't want any fucking favors."

He made a gesture of resignation by holding up both palms, said,

"Slow down, my friend. Don't bite the messenger."

I stood up, said,

"I'm not your friend and don't let me see you on my case again."

He laughed, said,

"The Greek gift."

I asked,

"What?"

"It refers to a chess sacrifice that is frequently deadly, i.e., the Wooden Horse at Troy. What they thought was a gift was a fatal attack."

I shook my head, said,

"Nobody talks sense anymore."

I moved to the door, fed up with them all. The bar guy called,

"Hey, Jack, who is on the green pound note?"

To appreciate silence
you kind of
need
first
to shut the fuck up.

I went to see the nun, Sister Maeve. It was she who introduced me to Marion and set me on the course of what seemed to be happiness.

The road to hell is paved with well-intentioned nuns.

Our friendship was odd, to say the least. She had asked for help on a Church mini crisis and, though I did sweet fuck-all, it got resolved and put me in good, if false, light.

You take the kudos when they fall.

She seemed to genuinely have great fondness for me. If anyone could help me salvage my love affair it was Maeve.

I purchased all her treats:

Black Forest gâteau,

Strawberry cheesecake,

And

Herterich handmade sausages.

She lived in a small house on Saint Francis Street, but a rosary from the Abbey Church.

Before, when I called on her, she would seem delighted.

This time?

Not so much.

She said,

"Oh, it's you."

Mmm.

I asked because I had to.

"May I come in?"

Grudgingly,

"Um, okay."

I handed over the gifts as she didn't ask me to sit.

Usually, she'd be all over those treats like delight in action but now left coldly on the table.

I asked,

"Is everything all right?"

I'm a PI, sensitive to these nuances.

Mainly I'm an asshole.

She was avoiding my eyes. I placed myself right in front of her face, put my hand on her shoulder, asked,

"What is it, Sister?"

Not using her Christian name seemed to snap her out of it, she gulped.

"Jack, I'm so sorry."

I was all concern, soothed.

"It's okay, really. Is it about Joffrey? I won't bring him to a pub again, okay?"

She did something she never had done. She got a bottle of whiskey, a brand not seen since the flood, Robin Redbreast, poured two healthy dollops into glasses with a blue sheen and the logo

OUR LADY OF GUADALUPE.

I doubt she knew this was the Madonna of the cartels. I didn't share, raised my glass, said,

"*Dia leat*" (God be with you).

She made a face as she sipped her drink, said,

"Oh, my Lord."

Not so much a prayer as a shock.

I could see her steel herself for whatever she had to tell, her knuckles white. She said,

"Marion is going back to Sean."

Sean? Who the fuck was *Sean*?

My blank face prompted her to add,

"Her husband."

Aw, fuck.

She asked,

"You didn't know?"

Like hello, take a wild freaking guess.

We had an unspoken agreement to leave the past alone, to take it from when we met. Like did I think Joffrey was an immaculate conception?

I said,

"I didn't know."

She went to touch my arm but I shook her off, said,

"I have to go."

Then I spotted a new item on her bureau. A gleaming white chess set. I asked,

"You play chess?"

She nearly smiled, said,

"Your friend brought it."

I was nearly afraid to ask but did, echoed,

"My friend?"

"Yes, Mr. Allen, a lovely man but I'm not sure I entirely knew what he meant."

"How do you mean?"

He said,

"Tell Jack he's touchable."

I had a Montblanc pen that I'd nicked from a lawyer. I bought a Moleskine diary from Mary in Hollands. She was, as always, just lovely in every way, said,

"'Tis great to see you, Jack."

I refused to allow that to lift my mood. Went to Richardson's pub at the very top of Eyre Square. It had been there for as long as I could remember but few people I knew were likely to be there. I got a boilermaker, a table at the rear, set out my fucked life.

Like this:

Marion was very likely a done deal.

The Fisher King, this *Silence* guy, who kept intruding in my life.

Tevis, what was the bloody gig with this dude?

Pierre Renaud, who'd had his sons murdered.

And what . . .

What the hell was I to do with this mess?

If I visualized a chessboard, it was thus basically a four-move gig.

A guy came over to my table, despite the whole vibe of *fuck off* I was emanating. Well dressed, tanned, expensive haircut, about my age but oh, oh so much better preserved.

He had a shot glass of something strong, sat, asked,

"Remember me, Jack?"

"No."

He nodded as if expecting nothing more, said,

"Jimmy Dolan. I sat beside you at school."

I gave him the look that is but a twitch away from a glare, asked,

"And?"

Flustered him as intended. He tried,

"Just, you know, I thought I'd say hello."

Looking like he now knew it was a very bad notion so I eased a bit, asked,

"How have you been, Jimmy Dolan?"

In Irish terms, you use a person's full name thus, it is as close to a slap in the mouth as it gets.

A slight smile, then,

"I'm in tires."

Did that require an answer that bore any relation to civility? I nodded sagely as if I'd read Booker-nominated titles. He said,

"It's not like I woke up one morning and thought, *Whoa,* I just gotta get into tires."

I felt a question was probably required about here, so,

"There's money in tires, is there?"

He stared for a moment, wondering if there was mockery. Then,

"Let me say, I've a nice home, place in the country, Barbados twice yearly."

Here, he shot his cuff to reveal a shiny Rolex, the new very slim one that, really, you'd be mortified to own let alone wear.

Continued:

"Two boys in the very best schools."

I wanted to shout,

"I know a guy with two boys in the river."

Instead, I went,

"The Irish new success story."

He stood up, went and got a round of drinks, came back, handed me a glass, asked,

"Jameson, right?"

His was a double, mine the lone shot, gulped his, swallowed with a grimace like in the movies, said,

"You'd think I'd be happy."

I actually thought almost nothing save *so what?*

I said,

"I should think so."

He scoffed, near spat,

"Like fuck."

I said,

"Fried liver."

He went,

"What?"

"It's a chess tactic, like the four-move checkmate, and it is a lethal one. The name comes from *dead as fried liver.*"

He said,

"I don't play fucking chess."

I stood up, finished my drink, said,

"And you wonder why you're not happy."

May 22, in Manchester at a concert for youngsters and teenagers, a suicide bomber killed twenty-two and seriously injured fifty-nine others.

There was a stunned horrific silence

'Round the world.

The next evening, Man United were playing against Ajax for the only trophy they had never won.

The heavens cut Manicheans some slack and they won by two goals.

The globe was now oh, so much smaller and so very, very dangerous.

On the street, a guy tried to sell me the newest craze, *fidget gadgets.* Designed to allow children to fidget.

How times had changed and oh, so utterly. When we were children, in that country no longer recognizable, we were warned on peril of our lives,

"Don't fidget."

A four-day heat wave hit the city and, of course, confused us. The guys in battered shorts, very white scrawny legs, thick socks, and, phew-oh, sandals.

A and E would be swamped with sunburn cases and heat-stroke. Ice-cream vans would make a small country's killing.

After twenty-five years, Guns N' Roses returned to Slane and it was even suggested that Axl Rose and Slash were talking to each other after decades of a feud. Murmurs of rehab and AA, sober living plus vegan tendencies slightly dented the old outlaw image.

Eighty-five thousand people were attending the concert with four hundred Guards on duty.

A guy asked me,

"Would you know offhand which page of the Bible tells you how to turn water into wine?"

At the height of the heat wave, a young man put his eight-month-old baby in the car, then went to work. *Forgot* the baby was there and went to his job.

Returned to the car after five hours to find the baby dead.

The Guards did not arrest him.

Donald Trump wept at the Wailing Wall in Jerusalem.

Across town, the pedophile Peter Boyne was putting the final touches to his plan to snatch Joffrey. He was in a state of high excitement. Laid out his materials:

Plastic ties

Chloroform

A long knife with serrated blade, not that he wanted to have to use this,

Wanted the goods in fine form.

He had memorized the school times and there was a window early morning as the boy went to meet the school bus.

He would wear black pants, black ski mask, and black sweatshirt. The last was tight, his bulk barely fitting it.

He hadn't washed the van—white, of course.

They are always white (see Patrick Hoffman's *The White Van*).

Dirt obscured the license plates. Not to mention the fact he was a lazy git who could barely wash himself.

Lately he had been in chat rooms dedicated to *man / boy love*. These were in the dark net where such items as

Weapons

Drugs

Passports

Were available.

Going deep a few weeks back, chugging Southern Comfort and emboldened, he'd gone to the electric website where *killing kids* was the gig.

It filled him with awe.

The Duke of Brunswick Defense

Then along came Harley.

Phew-oh.

Where to start with that?

The beginning, I guess.

I was outside Garavan's, the town hopping. Sunshine and buskers. If Galway had weather all year round there'd be no room for the locals. I was watching a small film unit, with a guy before the camera. He was tall, rangy, lanky, with a breadth of long blond hair, thinking,

He is the spit of the guy who was in the Nordic noir *Easy Money*, then went on to play the

Junkie

Punk

Recovering addict

In the American version of *The Killing*,

Which led to a breakout role in *House of Cards*.

What the hell was his name?

He spotted me, his face lit up, and he did that throat slash gesture that means kill the film.

He strode toward me, his fingers laced to make that frame scene beloved of media people. Ordered,

Nay, *commanded*,

"Don't move."

Then to the camera guy,

"Raoul, get Jack framed against the bookshop. It is fucking downright *iconic*."

I was thinking,

Hello, Jack?

He put out his hand, gushed,

"Harley Harlow's the name and documentaries are my game, and a privilege to meet Jack Taylor."

Said in Brit voice interspersed with American twang.

Then aside to Raoul,

"You are getting this, Raoul?"

I said, very quietly,

"Don't film me."

He threw up his hands in delight, near shrieked,

"Oh, God, so butch. I love it. You're even more . . . *primeval* than I dared to hope for. I could come right now."

WTF?

I asked,

"Who in hell are you?"

He did what might be described as the *Valley girl coy simper* (a horror all its own), asked,

"You're thinking I look like the guy in *The Killing*, am I right? Oh, I wish, Jose."

The name came to me.

Joel Kinnaman.

I put a finger to his mouth, said,

"Shut . . . the . . . fuck . . . up. Now, who are you?"

He pulled back in mock outrage, then smiled.

"We are Hard Productions, award-winning documentary makers, noted entry at Sundance with *Crystal Murder* in 2003."

I nearly smiled, albeit with bitterness writ large, echoed,

"*Hard*? Seriously, like a hard-core porno gig?"

He reached in his safari jacket (yes, the movie version) and took out an e-cig, vaped furiously, then grinned.

"Double entendre right there, Jack-o. It stands for Hit . . . and . . . Run . . . Documentaries. And that is our style: guerrilla tactics, in out, fast furious, like Clint makes his movies, no second takes."

Since Marion's call, I was back full-on smoking, reached for my pack of Major—yeah, those coffin nails—then a heavy silver Zippo from my days with Emerald, clunked that babe, lit up, ah . . .

He stared at the Zippo, drooled.

"So Waylon Jennings, you are going to love the title of this doc."

I decided to humor the lunatic, asked,

"Hit me."

He laughed, said to Raoul,

"I love this dude."

Then to me,

"*Gay Indian Nation*."

He couldn't be serious if he was what I think he was intending. Our new prime minister, a doctor, was

Gay

Indian.

I said,

"Good Lord, you can't say that."

He seemed puzzled, asked,

"Is your prime minister Indian?"

"Well, of Indian parents."

"And is he not of the light-of-foot persuasion?"

God, what a term. I said,

"Yes . . . but . . ."

He near roared.

"But me no buts. Aren't you Irish supposed to be fearless in your speech, as in Bob Geldof, Sean O'Casey?"

Why was I even trying to debate with this ejit? I asked,

"What is the doc about?"

Like I could give a tupenny fuck but anything to be shot of him.

He grabbed my shoulders with both hands, a very risky move. Said,

"You, you, Jack Taylor, are my subject, my quarry, my bête noire."

Sweet Jesus.

I said with absolute sincerity,

"You're shitting me."

He was on fire, started,

"But it's so perfect, the new broken Ireland, with a broken PI. I mean, you couldn't make this shit up, man."

I tried,

"Like that is going to fly, a PI in Galway?"

He mock-intoned,

"Oh, ye of little faith, am I not the dude who made a doc on an anorexic girl way down in the bayou, got tones of sepia and Daniel Woodrell in there, and it got nominated for the Golden Bear in Berlin?"

I kind of wanted to know, not hugely, but in there, asked,

"What did you call that?"

He paused, threw a look at Raoul who was lighting a cig, then said,

"*Pangs in the Bayou.*"

"Why?"

He seemed genuinely puzzled, said,

"Like hunger pangs, you know, anorexia?"

"I know what it is."

He slapped me on the shoulder, said,

"Lemma buy you a brew, Pilgrim."

Added,

"My treat. Your money's no good when you're in the company of the Harley."

Jesus, he actually said that.

I turned, went into Garavan's. He followed, as did the bold Raoul. Seamas, I hadn't seen in donkeys, was tending bar, greeted,

"I thought you were dead."

"No, I was in England."

He sighed, answered,

"Same thing."

Harley motioned to Raoul, *Keep frigging filming.*

He nigh leaped to the bar, ordered.

"Two boilermakers, my good fellow."

Seamas was never, ever anyone's *good fella.* Maybe shades of Behan's *The Quare Fellow.* But good? No way.

Harley added, in a snotty tone,

"You do know what a boilermaker is?"

Fuck.

I grabbed his arm, snarled,

"Rule number one: never antagonize the bar guy."

For one fleeting moment, something crossed Harley's face that showed there was something darker beneath the *hail-fella-well-met bullshit*, and, you know, that softened my view of him, not a lot, but in there.

The pints came and Seamas, God bless his Galway soul, deciding to play along, put the Jay in shooters, the shot glasses. Harley said,

"Let's do this thing."

As if we were heading into battle, which, in some ways, we were. He took the creamy top off the pint, then dropped the shot glass in.

It's all a movie.

Was I going to do similar? I knocked the shot back solo. Harley seemed crestfallen. I asked,

"How exactly is this doc going to go down?"

He had half his drink gone, and it seemed to agree with him as he smiled, said,

"It's already going down, partner."

I rubbed my fingers together, said,

"Cash."

Took some of my pint for effect, then,

"*Partner.*"

He said,

"Let's not mess this up with *finance.*"

I took out a ten, tip for Seamas, looked directly at Harley, said,

"Good luck with that."

Fucked off outa there.

There is a silence in a cemetery the very moments before the coffin is lowered into the ground, an all-pervading stillness, a hush that whispers on the barren wind, the very essence of tranquillity.

(Kiki Taylor, Jack's ex-wife)

The bland song "The Sounds of Silence"

Had been reinterpreted by a band named, appropriately enough,

Disturbed.

Channeling Metallica, it is a brutal, beautiful, nigh-biblical threat.

In the new version, a black-and-white video accompanies this; it could be a scene from a John Sayles movie.

Almost on its heels I heard

"Human."

The singer of this called himself

Rag 'n' Bone Man.

The wonderful thing about these ballsy singers is they are so far from the current range of *pretty boy* whiners. Made you feel hope in a Trump universe.

Then, less than two weeks after the Manchester horror, came a concentrated three-pronged attack in London, but the consolation at least was the police shot and killed the three lunatics in just eight minutes.

My phone rang. Owen, my friend in the Guards, said,

"Jack, Clancy has been hit by a car."

Superintendent Clancy, my nemesis.

I snapped,

"I didn't do it."

I could nearly see his guilty smile. He added,

"He is in hospital, in a coma."

I asked,

"You think I should bring him grapes?"

Pause.

Then,

"I think you should bring a solid alibi."

While I mulled this over, the phone rang again.

Tevis.

He said,

"Jack, my colleagues decided to do you a biggie, to show that Two for Justice has your best interests at play."

Oh, fuck, not good.

I asked,

"Why would they do that?"

He snorted as if suppressing a giggle, said,

"To ensure you leave the investigation of the twins' father alone."

I said nothing.

He pushed.

"Don't you want to know what they did?"

Not really.

I said,

"Sure."

"We settled a score from your past, an irritation that has plagued you down the years, and to think you once were friends."

Clancy?
I asked,
"Superintendent Clancy?"
Now he laughed, said,
"You'd think a Guard would be more careful on the road."
And hung up.
Each
Angel
> *Is*
>> *Terrible.*

This was the title of a quasi-memoir put out by Scott Harden.
A crime writer living along the canal. He was in his fifties but
looked older; an alleged stint in a South American jail had given
him preternaturally totally white hair.

Tall and thin to the point of perhaps illness but his olive skin
created a false sheen of health.

He liked to drink.

Jesus, don't we all?

His tipple of choice, and sales permitting, was tequila. Due
to the South American influence?

Who the fuck knows and, in truth, cares?

We weren't friends but we'd crossed paths often enough to
allow us to drink on occasion without sweating it. This time, we'd
met on the prom. He was staring out at the ocean, a practice I'd
enjoyed my own self. What did he see?

America?

Jail?

Failure?

He was dressed as always in battered brown leather jacket, dark jeans, off-white trainers. I thought,

"I could be looking at me *fein*" (myself).

He sensed me. I guess if you survive prison in a hellhole, your sense of preservation is acute. He greeted,

"'Tis yourself."

I answered,

"Buy you a pint?"

Not of tequila, no.

We went to Sally Longs, quiet midafternoon. I ordered the black and he opted for two bottles of Bud, no glass, explained,

"I like to turn out for the U.S. as they are the only gang to buy my books."

I asked,

"How's that going for you?"

He considered, then,

"If I put *girl* in the title, had a troubled but feisty female narrator, well, I'd have a shot."

We toasted with,

"*Sláinte amach.*"

And I asked,

"Will you go that route?"

He laughed, not from humor but something like weariness, said,

"It's that or a misery memoir."

I said,

"I'm reading Thomas Cook, *Tragic Shores.*"

He had the Bud bottle mid-lift, waited, asked,

"And?"

"Masterpiece."

He said,

"I'm going for a smoke."

Didn't ask, just stated it. That is very appealing. I joined him.
He produced a soft pack of Camels (they still sell those?) and
I smiled, said,

"The U.S., right? Your loyalty?"

"Fuck, no. A guy gave them to me."

He offered but I declined, said,

"I'm vaping."

He gave that odd smile, said,

"Is it on meself or does that sound just the tiniest bit gay?"

He lit up, coughed, exclaimed,

"God, they're stale."

"When did the guy give them to you?"

He thought for a moment, then said,

"A year ago."

I realized he had a way of speaking that you never were quite
sure if he was taking the piss or it was some private gig that
amused him alone.

He said,

"The guy? He told me he was a barrister."

"Okay."

"But turns out he meant barista."

Starbucks had recently opened in the Eyre Square center and was thriving. A phone shrilled. He took out one of the very old mobiles,

No camera

No video

No GPS

No paper trail.

He answered, went,

"Uh,

Huh,

Yeah,

Okay."

Finished the call. I said,

"You talk too much."

He looked like he might give me a hearty pat on the shoulder or a wallop in the face, said,

"Gotta boogie."

And took off.

I sat there and wondered if for writers a person wasn't ever *real*,

Simply part of the plot. A guy at the bar asked me,

"Was that that writer bollix?"

Which in Ireland is as near a left-field recognition as you will get. But okay, it pissed me off, so I snarled,

"Have you read his books?"
Got the incredulous look and this,
"They're stabbing books."
Argue that.
More and more, odd events triggered events from my past.
My father was a good, gentle man. How he ended up with my
walking bitch of a mother is a mystery. He never once laid a
finger on me. Which, nowadays, abuse seeming to be almost
mandatory, is indeed remarkable.
But my dear *mammie*?
Phew-oh, cunt on wheels.
I came home from school, I was about eleven, a hot dinner
and care was not the order of the day. She was waiting behind
the door and floored me with a wallop to my head, stood over
me with her weapon of choice, a thin nasty reed, with tiny
embedded studs.
No wonder the clergy loved her. She was their poster girl of
punishment, the embodiment of piety and pious posing.
She hissed, spittle leaking from the corners of her small, mean
mouth.
"Did you steal the rich tea biscuits?"
We had biscuits?
I burbled,
"No, cross my heart and hope to die."
She had systematically beaten me for a full four minutes.
I counted.

You think, four?

That's not so bad.

It is.

Immersed in a dark past, I told myself,

"Get some air, pal."

I did.

The sun was still beating down and hordes of Irish bewildered thronged Eyre Square. I sat at the top, near the John F. Kennedy memorial. God, we love them there Kennedys, even Teddy.

A woman, nicely dressed, with a solid bearing, holding the hand of a gorgeous little girl, dressed like Holly Hobbie. (Remember her? Little bonnet, cute booties, channeling Laura Ingalls Wilder.*)

The * is for "footnote"; if you want to go literary, have at least one footnote.

The woman approached, the little girl smiling hesitantly.

The woman.

Something in the way she moved.

She stood right in front of me, said,

"Gretchen, say hello to your father."

*From *Little House on the Prairie.*

If you go far enough
into
the past
you will meet
yourself
coming back.

(Galway drinking song lyric)

I stared at the woman, asked,

"Kiki?"

Oh, my sweet shocking Lord.

My ex-wife.

Though if you measure in time quantity it barely scraped under the legal wire.

After *the Guards,* such is how I see my dismissal from said force, I went to London.

Went to bits.

Living on Ladbroke Grove (not at all like in the Van Morrison song), and in some barely remembered haze, met and married a German professor of metaphysics. In her defense, she was even more into booze than me. I think she thought I was some sort of Behan manqué.

Two weeks and she was howling for divorce.

I had a beard as my hands shook too much to shave.

A child?

Really?

I thought,

What the fuck.

The chronology I figured would be about right.

KEN BRUEN

I think.

She asked,

"You do not remember me?"

In a tone that leaked a now recalled severity in her speech. Maybe it was a German thing to be so direct. I said,

"*Guten Tag, Gedichte und Briefe zweisprachig.*"

How I dredged that up, Christ knows.

But she liked it and, even better, so did the child.

Fuck, the insanity of the alkie mind-set. In my head I was already playing happy families. The child was staring at me with utter bewilderment. I asked in my dumb fashion,

"Does . . .

Does . . .

She

Speak

English?"

A fleeting irritated expression danced across Kiki's face. Now I remembered her intolerance of my ill-thought-out processes. She snapped,

"Gretchen was raised in New York where I got sober. She speaks three languages."

I nearly asked,

"Any of them civil?"

As Kiki spoke, the sleeve of her Barbour jacket rode up, showing a gold Rolex oyster on a nicely tanned arm. The Germans coming to Ireland have obviously heard of our *soft* rain as the first thing they pack is ye old royal *Barbour.*

Even the child sported a Rolex.

Fuck.

This retriggered the *happy family* shit, and mindful of Kiki's Ph.D. in metaphysics I said,

"The meta racket paying better than you'd expect."

Gretchen piped up,

"Mommy is a doctor for sick souls."

This, in an American twang. I wondered if maybe it was Teutonic humor.

Kiki said,

"My second husband is a very successful man."

Second.

What kind of floozy was she?

I asked,

"How long are you in town for?"

She patted the child's head and I for a split second wished it were me.

Madness.

She said,

"We must leave tomorrow for Berlin."

The *must* bearing all the gravitas of the German imperative.

Then, with a sad smile, she referenced the TV show we'd watched in our brief time, said,

"*Auf Wiedersehen, Pet.*"

As they turned to go, the child whispered in German to her.

I figured she wanted maybe a hug, asked,

"What did she say?"

"She asked why you are so old."

"Upon
  Some
     Midnights
         Clear"

(K. C. Constantine)

"They threw a dead dog into the hole after the consul's body."

Such are the end lines of Malcolm Lowry's
Under the Volcano.

Lines I always found shocking on so many levels. In the movie version, Albert Finney produced the best on-screen depiction of an alcoholic ever.

Such were my meanderings after discovering I had a daughter and, gee, I had all of ten minutes with her.

My cup fucking overflowed.

Across town, Joffrey was walking home from school.

He felt independent.

Didn't take any notice of the white van a few yards from him. As he approached, a fat man came quickly around the side, grabbed him, pushing a cloth over his mouth, a cloth that smelled of hospitals. In seconds he was limp.

Peter Boyne was sweating profusely, but joy mixed with adrenaline coursed through his body. He muttered,

"Oh, my beauty."

He slid the side door open, threw the body inside, didn't dare look around but moved quickly, got in the driver's seat, and slowly pulled away. He hit the music deck. Queen blasted forth,

"We Will Rock You."

"Too fucking right."

He shouted.

Punched the air in victory.

As he disappeared in traffic, a lone schoolbag lay on the path, like a discarded wish.

In Irish folklore three kinds of silence are identified:
Silence through fear,
Silence through choice,
Silence of compassion.

"I only understood the third."

(Tevis)

Lockdown.

In a whirl of grief, rage, frustration,
I barricaded myself in the apartment.
"Some are born to endless night."
My mind was a cesspool of
Remorse
Recrimination
Revolt.

Any word beginning with *R*, especially revulsion. Blocked out the world. My phone turned off. Sipping on Jay, trying to measure out how drunk I intended to get. Watched
Fargo 3.

David Thewlis, in a performance to rival Billy Bob Thornton in series one. This was indeed the time of Noah Hawley, his novel *Before the Fall* winning a shitload of awards, his early books reissued, and *Legion* receiving rave reviews in its first season.

A line from his early novel *The Punch* spooling in my head:
"Different bullets, same gun."

The Hound of Heaven was no longer simply snapping at my heels but in full sit on my chest, heavy as death. I read a long account of the failed attempt by Andrew O'Hagan to write the bio of Assange, then followed that with a book of the twelve marines who guarded Saddam in his last months before he was hanged.

Nearly laughed in an insane fashion that Saddam had a special liking for Mary J. Blige.

You mutter,

"Like dude, seriously?"

Reread the classic horror by Anne Siddons, *The House Next Door.*

Then I turned my phone on and hell reared up on its ferocious legs and howled.

I heard hysteria, writ large, the weeping and keening of tears. I was as aforementioned, not in the best set of patience, snarled,

"Cut the drama, I can't hear you."

Marion.

A moment as she composed herself, then,

"It's Joffrey, they've taken him."

WTF?

I took a second to focus, then did the ice gig, asked,

"Who? Who took him?"

"We don't know. He's been missing for three days."

I managed to stay on the cool vibe, asked,

"Where are you?"

"I'm staying with Maeve. I flew home as soon as I heard. Oh, God, Jack, what will I do?"

Like I had a clue but the even tone was working, so I said,

"Come over here. I will get right on it."

"Oh, thank you, Jack, and I'm sorry the way I spoke to you last time."

Me, too.

But

"Just get here. I'll be making calls."

What, I'd call the Guards?

Gave me time to shower, clean up the debris of my bender, did some lines of coke to fly right, wore a crisp new white shirt, the camouflage of the seasoned drinker. It near blinded me in its brightness and those fucking pins they put in them left my fingers shredded. The shakes, sure, but the coke was kicking its ass.

As I did the mop-up, I saw the cover of the DVD.

Abraham Lincoln, Vampire Hunter.

Yeah.

Shows how nuts I'd been for those lost days. It was brilliantly bonkers and had Dominic Cooper whom recently I'd watched as *Preacher,*

With Joe Gilgun

Giving a master class in demonic craziness, playing, wait for it, *Irish vampire who was also a dope fiend and boozer.*

You don't need to be way out there to appreciate these dark insane series but it doesn't hurt.

Maybe I'd watch

Pride and Prejudice and Zombies.

Finally, a way to watch Jane Austen without being bored shitless.

Then, oh Lord,

A sheet of paper with this in barely legible writing:

Kiki Taylor
Room 37
Meyrick Hotel
Ph. 577821

Two feelings colliding:

Horror at what I might have said if I did call her.

Kind of fucked-up delight that she still used my name.

How utterly lame was that?

I checked myself in the mirror, the white shirt did help but the eyes . . .

Seriously fucked. I couldn't answer the door in shades.

Could I?

She'd think Bono's dad was staying with me.

I rang Owen, my Guards contact. He was not pleased, growled,

"The fuck, Jack? You can't ring me every time you have a problem."

I had to rein in my urge to blast him out of it.

I said,

"You don't even know why I'm calling. It might be to ask *how you doing?*"

He sniggered, went,

"Yeah, like that would ever happen. I'm like the cop Dennis in *The Rockford Files*, used only for info."

I was surprised he was familiar with James Garner but then guys of a certain age . . .

I asked,

"How are you, Owen, how are the family? The children must be big now."

Deep sigh, then,

"My wife left me and we never had a family."

Ah.

Before I could work any more insincerity, he said,

"It's about that kid, right?"

"How'd you know I'd be asking?"

Bitter laugh.

"You're riding his mother."

I was nearly shocked at the casual crudity, but I asked,

"Any developments?"

He went quiet, said, after hesitation,

"It's four days now."

I tried,

"But you are looking?"

"The boy is dead, Jack."

Pause.

"Or worse."

Fuck.

I asked,

"Any leads?"

He sighed, said,

"All the usual suspects and some new names the public provided. There are even more crazies out there than you'd imagine."

I heard him draw a deep breath. He asked,

"What's up with you, boyo? You're four days late to the party. What's that about? Didn't you give a fuck until now?"

Bollocks.

I tried,

"Um, I was attempting my own inquiries."

Hoped to God that would fly.

It didn't.

He laughed without a trace of humor, near spat,

"Jesus wept. You were on the piss. I fucking don't believe it. Seriously? That's a new low even for you, Taylor."

Hung up.

I muttered,

"All in all, I think it went okay."

The doorbell chimed.

Marion.

Looking like the wreck of many Hesperuses.

She didn't quite fall into my arms but did wobble in near faint.

I led her into the flat, got her a solid drink.

She took the drink, tears rolled down her cheeks, made a very soft *plink* against the rim of the glass. What could I say?

The utterly lame,

"It's going to be all right."

Yeah, that would fly.

I said,

"It's going to be all right."

She gulped the drink, a moment, and then color returned to her cheeks.

When mega-comfort was necessary, the very devil poisoned my soul. I asked,

"How is Sean?"

She was stunned, if more stunning were even possible. She near whimpered,

"Who?"

"Your husband, you know, the guy you forgot to mention."

Fuck.

It looks bad.

It was. She got to her feet, swayed.

The doorbell rang.

She said very quietly,

"Maybe it's news of Joffrey."

It wasn't.

Kiki.

The women stared at each other, not in friendly fashion.

Marion asked,

"Who's she?"

She said,

"I'm his wife."

How valour clothed in courtesies
Brings down the haughtiest house.

(*The Angel in the House*,
Coventry Patmore, 1823–96)

I found myself in Freeney's, a quiet pub on Quay Street. The tourists stroll right on by, probably misled by the fishing tackle in the window. You get your pro barmen here.

Not quite surly but definitely not big greeters. You get a nod, that's it, but the service is excellent and the pint is pure quality. The sort of pint that is so fine it seems a sin to disturb the perfect creamy head.

It stocks Midleton whiskey, a brand but a prayer away from Jameson. The selling point, the clincher for me, is nobody can find you there.

Almost.

I was midway through the black, with just a hint of the whiskey, when Tevis sat in the chair opposite me.

He asked,

"Are you a death metal headbanger?"

I looked at him with suppressed fury, snarled,

"Do I look like I am?"

He smiled, shook his head, then,

"You're a piece of work, Monsieur Taylor. Two women, count 'em, one a wife and the other . . . fiancée? Or significant other? What puzzles me is the nature of your game—apologies to the Rolling Stones—how you manage to piss them all off. Is it love 'em and dump 'em?"

I said,

"How you know so freaking much about my life is not only creepy but becoming seriously threatening."

The barman brought him a tall glass of sparkling water. Unheard of.

To receive table service here . . . I was fucked if I'd ask him how. He said, holding the glass up to the light,

"Vodka and sparkling water, a surprisingly refreshing if, alas, somewhat gay beverage."

I said, very slowly,

"You need to think carefully how much it is you want to annoy me."

He leaned over, gave me a playful punch to my shoulder. I asked myself,

"Is he stone fucking mad?"

He said,

"You're thinking, am I mad? But let me ask you this. How much would you like to be the guy who saves the boy?"

I stared at him in complete astonishment.

He said,

"Impressive, huh? How much would your intended be grateful if you brought back that snotty little fuck of hers?"

All I had was,

"How?"

He stood up, said,

"It's a biggie but you mull it over for, like, two minutes."

He went to the bar, got drinks and an armful of Tayto. Came back, mega-smile in place, dumped the lot on the table, muttered,

"Who's the daddy?"

Raised his glass, clinked mine, said,

"Here's the heroes."

My turn to lean. I did, put my index finger bang in the middle of his forehead, said very quietly,

"Who has the boy?"

He pulled back, a fleeting dance of fear across his face, said,

"A pedophile, and Two for Justice has the location."

I was outraged, wanted to spit with anger, asked,

"That fucking lunatic, the ex-soldier or who the fuck ever he calls himself, the Quietness?"

He put up his hand, to shush me.

"The *Silence*. It's important to get the terms right, especially if you want his um . . . assistance."

I tried to dial it down, asked,

"This . . . guy . . . knows where the child is, even after four days and is, what, negotiating with me?"

Tevis tut-tutted. I mean he actually made the sound, said,

"You need to tone it down, fella, else I walk and kiss the boy good-bye."

Later, I'd kill the fuck, asked,

"What does he want?"

He gave a conciliatory smile, said,

159

"Better. Now to give yourself some breath to chill, hop on up there, get me another one of these refreshing drinks."

Was he serious?

I asked,

"You want me to ask for that punkish drink?"

He nodded, then,

"Time is a-running, lad."

The barman responded with a huge smile, said,

"Gay rights, eh?"

I brought the drink back, sat, waited.

Tevis rummaged among the bags of crisps on the table, selected Shamrock with cheese and onion, pulled the bag open, put a fistful in his mouth, then, between noisy chews, managed,

"Call them there crisps chips in America."

I said,

"I'll do whatever it takes to save the boy."

He finished the chips & crisps, said,

"That's the spirit. Two for J is very loyal to its, um, *clients*, and their protection is vital to the ongoing, so it is felt that even though you are a mess, an alkie mess . . ."

He paused,

Winked,

Said,

"Not my words or indeed even sentiments,

But

You do tend to somehow get results and so your word is needed that no investigation into their affairs will happen."

I said,

"I give my word."

"Bravo. Here is what will happen. The boy will be delivered to your apartment, you will ring the mommy, be the hero."

"How do I explain the rescue?"

"Lie. Lie big."

He got up, smiled. I said,

"Your name, I figured it . . . from Walter Tevis, who wrote perhaps the best novel on chess, *The Queen's Gambit*."

He wasn't fazed, said,

"You need to learn *forks, pins, and skewers*."

And he was gone.

Forks, pins, and skewers are some of the sneakiest tricks you can use against your opponent. These tactics will lead to defeating your enemy.

(*Beginning Chess*)

I was sitting in my apartment, not drinking, waiting on the call about the boy.

I'd popped a Xanax but a dread had settled in my stomach, not helped by the cigarette I'd smoked.

Ring.

Put me through the roof. I answered, heard Tevis.

"The lad will be delivered to your front door in minutes. *Do not wait outside the door.* You will then bring him to the hospital, call his mommy, and, for the Guards, you will say you got a call from a source to go to Eighteen, Water Alley, off Devon Park. You found the door open and the child unconscious on an air mattress. The occupant had fled. You immediately rushed him to the A and E. Got it?"

Silence.

Then, irritated,

"Got it?"

"I'm only partially deaf. Is the boy okay?"

A nasty chuckle, then,

"Okay? He's fucked is what he is."

Click.

Five long minutes, I counted every damn second, then my doorbell rang. Opened to find the boy unconscious on a sleeping bag, dressed in a white tracksuit, bruising on his face. I called a cab, then his mother, who was hysterical. I said,

"I found Joffrey, am rushing him to the hospital."

Deep intakes of breath, then she asked,

"Is he alive?"

"Yes, a bit banged up but he'll be fine."

Yeah, right.

I clicked off, picked up the boy, blood congealed on the bottom of the boy's pants. I daren't think on that, got him to the cab, managed to ignore the driver's barrage of questions.

The hospital was pandemonium. A hysterical grateful Marion, suspicious Guards, worried doctors. Within a short time the press arrived and the Guards had to extract me from a babble of reporters.

Whisked to Mill Street, the Guards' headquarters. Shoved, pushed into the office of the new superintendent.

A woman.

In her late forties, with blond hair tied in one of those severe buns that screams: I am not a sexual being. Her face had the requisite hard edges that cautioned,

"Do not even think about fucking with me."

She said,

"I am Mary Wilson."

A thug / sergeant was right behind me, breathing curry chips on my neck. I said,

"I didn't even know you left the Supremes."

Bang.

From the thug.

It hurt.

I said,

"If this moron hits me again, I will come across the desk and he'll have to beat me senseless to subdue me. Then how will the press like that the boy's rescuer had the shit kicked out of him?"

An eye signal to the ape, who moved to my side.

She asked,

"How did you find the boy?"

"Through the very grace of God."

I managed to move fast to my side to avoid the intended heavy blow to my ribs.

Wilson said,

"Your story reeks. If I find you are connected in any way you are in deep shit. Now get out."

As they pushed me to the door, I managed,

"Was Diana Ross really a diva?"

The press surrounded me, a gallon of questions until I managed to get into a cab, told the driver,

"McSwiggans."

As I got out, reached for my wallet, the driver said,

"No charge. You're a hero."

Fuck.

Silence
is
the
last
dance
of
the
disenchanted.

Michael Ian Allen.

They called him the *Silence.*

Meaning, he was usually the last thing you ever heard.

He was the only child of an Irish mother, American father, grew up in Watertown, Boston.

Quiet

Studious

Religious.

A Catholicism verging on fundamentalism instilled in him a fierce passion. He seemed destined for the priesthood but that other organization the Marines claimed him first.

He was a fine soldier, if not outstanding.

Until

Two patrols in Fallujah.

Both patrols were wiped out. He was the sole survivor—if just still breathing counted as life.

His initials had been almost a foreboding.

Some essential part of him had been MIA.

Chess and a warped sense of assisting those who were unable to help themselves lodged in what had been his soul. On leave, he had

2

4

J

Tattooed on his arm.

He wasn't entirely sure what his mission was until by chance he read an article about a man who tormented his family, received a slap on the wrist from the court.

"*Pawns.*"

He thought.

Victims who had no recourse to justice.

He'd be their advocate. His sense of definition varied from going after a man who beat his son in a supermarket to a bully who taunted a fat girl on the street. A crash of sounds roared in his head, the explosion of the Humvee.

With that first doomed patrol to the shrieks of the second as a mortar fired on them. Such times he physically shook his head to plead for ease.

A brief visit to the West of Ireland, land of his mother's people, led to a chance encounter with Pierre Renaud, who had come across Allen curled in a terrorized ball on the shores of Lough Corrib. Renaud had sat with him and gently soothed him down to a quiet green platform and whispered to him,

"*Le silence est magnifique.*"

A rare confluence of events:

Kindness

The soft words in a soft French

Compassion

Created

A jellying of benevolent quiet in the mind of Michael Allen.

Renaud had gone further . . . provided a small cottage in the wild of Connemara.

Many weekends the duo spent fishing, hunting, and just finding a solace in each other's company. One late Sunday evening, the men, tired from a day of hiking along the mountain trails, sat outdoors, sipping pure poteen, a turf fire fresh from the very bog they had traversed, when Allen said,

"You seem troubled, my friend."

Renaud, prodding the fire into a blaze, said,

"My sons plan to kill me."

He explained years of rebellion, bad behavior, insufferable attitudes, resulting in the twins' becoming obsessed with the Menendez brothers. Renaud thought they were just adding another layer of abuse to irk their father.

They had the books, documentaries on the trial and eventual jailing of the two young killers. Mocking their father with comments like

"The difference is we won't get caught."

Their mother, a drunk, refused to see or heed anything that was less than one hundred percent proof. He had managed to find a way to live that had him work every hour he could until . . .

Until.

He was searching the garage for old tax returns when he came across two brand-new shotguns.

Allen had listened with no interruptions.

When Renaud finally wound down, he was weeping softly. Allen asked,

"What do you want to do?"

A sudden wave of anger crossed Renaud's face. He spat,

"I want them to go away."

So it was.

Supports available

If in CRISIS please call:

Your local G.P.

Samaritans (24/7)
Freephone: 116 123

SUPPORTS

Text about it (24/7)
Text free: 50808

INFORMATION

www.yourmentalhealth.ie
YourMentalHealth (HSE) 24/7 info line
Freephone: 1800 111 888

www.citizensinformation.ie

www.hse.ie

Hello
HOW ARE YOU?

Mental Health Ireland

Visit our website:

www.HelloHowAreYou.info

Say **Hello** and ask: **How are you?**

Hello
HOW ARE YOU?

Mental Health

H	**e**	**l**	**l**	**o**
HELLO	ENGAGE	LISTEN	LEARN	OPTIONS
Say Hello and ask How are you?	Engage with the person	Actively listen to the person	Learn about the person & how they are feeling	Give time to talk through options

All islanders, no matter what their ethnicity,
live with a certain kind of longing.

(John Straley)

Harley, the documentary maker, was frustrated.

He was sitting in the Quays, on his second vodka, staring at Raoul, his camera guy. Raoul was, in fact, the whole crew.

The filming had been going well. He'd hired Jimmy Norman Media to get some very fine aerial shots of Galway at night. Norman Media used drones to huge effect.

Harley had been impressed but hid it from Jimmy lest he wanted payment then. Harley had perfected the fine art of never

Ever

Paying anybody.

He'd told Jimmy,

"Soon as the American money hits, you're first to be paid."

Jimmy had smiled, used to Galway shenanigans, said,

"No problem. I'll hold on to the footage until then."

Fuck,

Thought Harley.

There was American interest. A film about a broken-down PI in the West of Ireland, what was not to love? Harley had engaged the Galway singer-songwriter to compose a score for the doc. Marc Roberts had been easygoing and didn't demand cash up front.

Don Stiffe, another in-demand singer, had expressed interest but Don hailed from Bohermore, so he wasn't writing anything until he had a contract.

Locals had been great, happy to talk about Taylor, and Harley had got a ton of stuff on exploits, mostly false.

The Guards?

Not so much.

Had told Harley in no uncertain terms,

"Fuck off."

He wished Raoul had caught that on camera.

But best of all, the freaking money hook, Taylor, was now a bona fide hero.

You believe that luck?

Saved a snatched young boy.

Gold.

Pure guaranteed white gold.

Save

Taylor was unavailable.

As

Harley yet again laid out his frustration to Raoul, he noticed Raoul was not listening but watching as a man headed determinedly toward them. He was dressed in black jeans, black sweatshirt, and moved with a sure ease. His blond hair was cut in the buzz style, giving his face a granite look. He reached their table, said to Raoul,

"Get lost."

Raoul, accustomed to angry creditors, went without a word. The man took his stool, faced Harley, stared directly at him. Harley, uncomfortable, tried some East Brooklyn hard, said,

"Help you, fella?"

The man smiled, said,

"I'm Michael Allen."

Harlow shrugged, the vodka giving him some artificial spunk, said,

"So what?"

His phone beeped and he reached for it.

Allen's hand snapped out, gripped Harley's wrist. Allen said,

"Not now."

Harley, shaken, tried,

"You know who you're fucking with, buddy?"

Allen leaned real close, near whispered,

"You are what we used to call back home

A huckster

Flimflam man

Grifter.

But that's okay. Your Micky Mouse operation could use a major jolt."

Harley sensed opportunity, so went,

"Tell me more."

The bar guy, who was already lured by Harley's claim to celebrity, had watched the proceedings and now moved quickly. Strode over, put a hand on Allen's shoulder, addressed Harley,

"Everything under control here, Mr. Harlow?"

Letting a nice shade of hard dribble over his tone.

Without a movement, Allen said,

"You have twenty seconds to remove your hand and ten to scuttle back to the bar and get me a sparkling water."

You work in bars, especially on a hopping street like Quay, you know when to exercise caution. This was such a moment. He withdrew his hand and moved back to the bar. He poured a long glass of water from the tap, added Fairy washing-up liquid to get the bubbles and hopefully poison the bollix.

Walked back, plonked the glass down in front of Allen, winked at Harley.

Allen said,

"Taste it."

The bar guy was thrown, muttered,

"I don't do sparkling water."

Allen said,

"Neither do I, but you will drink that."

There it was.

Plain as day.

Implied violence. The bar guy stepped back. Allen turned, looked at him, said,

"Hey, just pulling your chain."

The sound of a cold humor was even more sinister than the outright threat.

As the chastened bar guy retreated, Allen threw,

"Soon as I find out where you live, I'll drop by, we'll have us a *sparkling* old time."

Then turned to Harley, asked,

"Where was I?"

Harley wanted to cry, just straight out bawl. He said,

"You were mentioning an opportunity?"

Allen smiled, asked,

"An exclusive, a hook to get the U.S. in on the project, an interview with the sicko who snatched the boy."

Harley saw the lure of that but,

"Will the Guards permit an interview?"

Allen continued the weird smile, said,

"The Guards don't currently have him."

Harley worked the angles, didn't see it, asked,

"Is he out on bail?"

Allen waited a beat, then,

"Peter Boyne is presently staying with me."

Harley echoed,

"Peter?"

"Indeed, Peter Boyne, and, if I say so, very keen to, how do you say, *spill the beans.*"

The
Summer
of
the
Black
Swan

A good summer in Galway is as rare as integrity. That July

The arts festival

The Galway races

And the black swan.

She appeared in the Claddagh Basin, and speculation was she'd come from South Africa. Not so much credence given there. She drew massive crowds and seemed content to accept food from the onlookers. Even walked on the shore to the delight and apprehension of children.

The other swans ignored her, not big on prima donnas. I watched her glide along the water and a tinker woman said,

"*Nil rud maith ag teacht*" (Nothing good is coming).

I thought,

So what else is new?

Asked her,

"Why's that?"

She looked at me, stated,

"*Ta tusa an mac* Taylor" (You're the Taylor boy).

I nodded, she said,

"A black swan is black luck."

I stared at her, asked,

"Really?"

More than a hint of disbelief lining my tone.

She took my hand. Spat in the palm, said,

"*Anois ta tu bheannacht*" (Now you are blessed).

I knew that gig, reached for my wallet, but she was gone. I looked 'round for her but she'd glided away as silent as the swan. I looked at my palm but it was dry. I said,

"I need a drink."

Pierre Renaud, the father of the murdered twins, was found hanging from a tree in his fine garden.

No note.

The belief was he'd been overcome by grief. I was in Garavan's on my first pint when Tevis arrived. Dressed in a good suit, linen lightweight, with a very sporty straw boater.

I said,

"Very Gatsby."

He ordered a small vodka, slimline tonic, said,

"Another sad bastard."

"Fitzgerald?"

He took a tentative sip. Then,

"No, I meant Renaud. You might say he had a bad *heir* day."

I'd heard about the death, said,

"Guilt?"

He gave a nasty chuckle, said,

"More a case of qualms."

Looked at him, got the nasty smile. He said,

"Ol' Pierre decided he couldn't live with what he'd done, so he was going to confess."

"Did he?"

Tevis finished his drink, contemplated another, said,

"Well, Allen felt there was another option."

I wasn't sure where this was going but didn't like the sense of it, asked,

"You mean he hung him?"

He recoiled in mock horror, said,

"What a nasty chain of thought you have."

Then he changed tack, asked,

"How is that Sophie's choice gig going for you?"

I had a fair idea of what he meant but feigned ignorance, asked,

"What are you on about?"

"Your wives? Or wife and concubine? Who'd you choose, the one with the kid? Oh, no, they both have those."

He gave an evil chuckle, said,

"One of those kids is, how do you say, shop-soiled."

I hit him fast and dirty, so fast he didn't actually fall down but it rocked his head like a seizure. No one in the pub seemed to have noticed. I leaned in, steadied him, and whispered,

"You have a real shitty mouth."

It took him a few moments to orient himself, then,

"Cheap shot, Jack. I thought you were better than that."

I got to smile, said,

"You thought wrong."

He glanced around the pub, said,

"Gee, not any of those fuckers realize I was just assaulted."
I said,
"Oh, they realize. They just don't give a fuck."

Harley and Raoul were waiting for Michael Allen outside Jurys
hotel, at the bottom of Quay Street. Raoul was wary of the
whole gig, said,
"What if this guy just offs us both?"
Harley, determined to be upbeat, said,
"Long as you get it on film."
Raoul went,
"Huh?"
Harley pointed to the swans, said,
"Instead of moaning, you could be over there getting some
footage of the black swan."
Raoul, vaguely interested, asked,
"As a noir metaphor?"
Harley snapped,
"How many times have I explained to you the difference
between an indie and a cult director?"
Raoul asked,
"Does either of those guys ever pay the camera crew?"
A white van rolled up, stopped. Allen leaned out, said,
"All aboard the magic bus."
Harley muttered,
"White van. What a cliché."

They piled in. Allen burned rubber.

As Harley and Raoul tried to find a seat in the rear of the van, Allen shouted,

"Mind what you touch, that's a crime scene."

As they sped up Grattan Road, the van braked suddenly, a group of hippie / monk-clothed people snaked across the road. Harley asked,

"Who the fuck are they?"

Allen sneered,

"The apostles of apocalypse."

Harley nudged Raoul to begin filming. Allen added,

"Euro trash, their trust funds crashed, so now they chant doom and end of days."

As Allen revved up, he said,

"Soon as I get some free time, I'm going to give them a taste of Armageddon."

Harley noticed there was no humor in that statement. The van continued out beyond Spiddal, turned into a small lane, pulled up outside a bungalow.

Allen jumped out, displaying the controlled force of his fitness. Harley followed him into the house. In the front room, bare save for two hard back chairs, a fat man in only his underpants was tied to one chair, sweating heavily. A fading bruise under one eye was the only sign of violence.

He stared at Harley.

Allen said,

"Meet Peter Boyne, child molester and failed kidnapper."

Boyne said nothing.

Allen indicated the other chair, said,

"You sit there, ask anything you want, and your camera guy can set up as he likes."

They did so. Raoul whispered to Harlow,

"This is like seriously fucked up."

Allen said,

"I'll be outside milking the cows."

To the baffled looks of all three, he added,

"Come on guys, cows? Really?"

But he did leave.

Harley got himself in interview mood, channeling what he thought of as his Cronkite tone. Boyne stared at him with dull curiosity.

Harley asked,

"State your name, please."

"Peter Boyne."

"Occupation?"

Raoul whispered,

"Kiddie hawk."

Boyne said,

"Lollipop man."

Harley nearly guffawed. It was like the title of a Stephen King short story. He went,

"What?"

"I help the children cross the road safely."

He said this without a trace of irony. Harley was delighted, and he pushed.

"And do you abduct them after they are safely across?"

Boyne looked offended, near shouted,

"I don't abduct children."

There was a silence as all digested this. Allen appeared behind Boyne, said to Harley,

"Don't adjust your set. This is a temporary glitch."

He walloped Boyne twice across the head, said,

"Play nice or you don't walk out of here."

Boyne tried to turn to look at him, whined,

"You'll never let me go."

Allen moved to the front of Boyne, hunkered down, leaned on Boyne's knees, said,

"Trust, Pete buddy, we got to have trust, else I take out your left eye. How would that be?"

Boyne nodded. Allen stood, did those neck stretches so beloved of deskbound yuppies, said,

"We're good to go."

Harley, shaken, began again.

"Um, when did you discover your, um, taste for, um, younger people?"

Allen moved, slapped Harley on the head, shouted,

"Seriously? This is your hard-core style? Ask him why he fucks kids!"

Harley pulled himself together, asked,

"How many children have you molested?"

Boyne just stared at him.

Raoul said,

"God sakes, this is not good."

Allen said,

"We need some snap, some pizazz."

He reached to his back, pulled out a Glock, racked the slide, moved to Boyne, asked,

"Snuff movie, anyone?"

If you have experienced utter silence
where the only sound is the steady beat
of your heart
it is nigh impossible to
readjust to mayhem.

(Sister Maeve)

Harley was busy. Very.

In anticipation of the coming success, he'd checked into the top floor of the Meyrick, said to the manager,

"Expect the world press to descend on this hotel in the next few days. You, my friend, are going to be very busy."

Ordered champagne and began phoning top TV outlets in the States, hinting at the explosive material he had. Looked around, shouted,

"Raoul, the fuck are you? Bring me a drink."

No Raoul.

Harley hung up on a West Coast hotshot, a nagging feeling starting in his gut. He saw Raoul's knapsack, rummaged through it. No film.

No film!

But there was a note.

"Dear shithead,
You like to lecture at length about your art.
The art of cinema.
Here's real art for you.
The guy with the film is the artist,
The guy holding the bag is
Fucked."

Harley's scream could be heard all the way down to the lobby.

* * *

195

The Galway races.

A week of utter madness, the pubs open until two in the morning, like the city went on the piss. Serious drinkers lay low; this was the time of messers. Apprentice drinkers who got loud and obnoxious.

I was in what civilized folk term a *quandary.*

Marion and / or Kiki.

I had met with Marion who, alas, wasn't all that grateful for my apparent rescue of her son. I asked,

"How is the little lad doing?"

She said,

"Like you care."

Jesus.

I wasn't seeing a whole rosy future here. I tried,

"I was glad to be able to help get him back."

Low shot, I know, but, hey, we weren't playing fair here. She said,

"I feel if we had never met you, this wouldn't have happened."

Fucking outrageous, right?

I said,

"That is not only untrue but it's downright offensive."

She went with the other weapon.

"Were you ever going to mention your wife and . . ."

Pause.

"*Child?*"

Time to fold.

Did I go dirty and mention her husband?

I asked,

"And your husband?"

Kiki.

I met her for a drink in Garavan's. I ordered a pint and she said,

"How typical of you, Jack. You know I'm in the program and yet you meet me in a pub."

Aw, fuck.

I had no energy after Marion. I asked,

"How is my daughter?"

She looked at me with a far distance from affection, asked,

"You even remember her name?"

I could have mustered some defense but, instead, I drained my pint, said,

"Have a great life."

Got the fuck out of there.

I walked along the canal, wondering if it was deep enough to drown myself. A guy was fishing and I stopped to watch. He was intent on the task, then said,

"Jack Taylor."

I asked,

"I know you?"

He felt a tug on the line and reeled in a large eel, took the hook out then released it, said,

"Stocks are low."

Then,

"You helped my old man out some years ago."

Well, finally some brightness.

He asked,

"You a betting man?"

I said,

"I'm not against it."

He said,

"There's a horse running at Galway today, the two forty-five, everything about him

Trainer

Jockey

Owner

Is local.

He's running against some very fancy horses. Like you, a lone voice against the big boys. His name is Pateen. He's all heart and endurance."

"Thank you."

I went to turn away and he added,

"Put a decent wager. Act like you believe."

I was on my way when he said,

"You know they say, *You learn more from a loss than a win?*"

"I've heard that."

He gave a very small smile, said,

"That's horseshit."

I put an indecent amount on the horse. He was 20–1.

He won.

I was heading down Forster Street with my substantial winnings when a small shop caught my interest. Near to the Puckeen pub, it had a variety of Galway souvenirs displayed. At the very back of the items I saw a black swan.

An omen, I thought.

Of what, I had no idea.

Bound to be a metaphor, at least.

I went in and the owner was a quick study in hostility. Without saying a word, he conveyed the notion I was a shoplifter. I said,

"The black swan, I'd like to buy it."

He stared at me, said,

"We don't have any white ones."

What?

I said,

"I don't want a white one."

His body shifted as if "*How much more aggravation can one man endure?*"

He said,

"The Galway swans are white."

God almighty.

I said,

"There's a black one there now."

He muttered,

"Sure."

But made no sign of moving.

I asked,

"So can I purchase the black one or not?"

He reluctantly got it, blew some dust off it, said,

"Thirty euros."

I was in some new realm of Monty Python so decided to go with it, asked,

"How much do you charge for the white ones?"

He took a step toward me. Was I going to end up wrestling with a shopkeeper on the floor of his shop?

He snarled,

"You're a bit of a smart-arse."

I said,

"As opposed to an actual customer?"

I threw the money on the counter, picked up the now controversial swan, said,

"You're probably overwhelmed with return shoppers."

And was out of there.

I headed up toward the square. A wino asked me for a few quid so I handed over some notes. I still had the swan, unwrapped, in my hand. He said,

"Funny, I always thought them birds were white."

*   *   *

I got back to my flat and, not for the first time, missed how no little pup would be waiting to welcome me. I shook my head to rid myself of the memory of the wonderful dog I had.

Was into the flat when I realized I was not alone. A man was standing against the window, staring out at the ocean. He seemed completely at ease, said,

"Hell of a view."

Turned to face me.

Tall, with a buzz cut, dressed in fatigues, a face that was nearly remarkable in its blandness. A suppressed energy danced around him. He said,

"I'm Michael Allen."

I said,

"The psycho."

He shrugged, said,

"Not an auspicious beginning to our meeting."

I said,

"It's not a meeting when you break into my flat."

He saluted, said,

"I didn't break anything."

Pause.

"Yet."

I gave him a long look, said,

"Time to pack up whatever nonsense you're peddling and fuck off."

He smiled, said,

"Harsh."

I had been rationing cigarettes in between vapings and reached for one now, fired up, said,

"Spill whatever it is."

He said,

"I thought a little gratitude might be forthcoming."

I said,

"You knew where the boy was being held but did nothing for three days."

He let out a deep sigh, said,

"Let me demonstrate something for you."

Crossed the room and in a split second flipped me on my back, his shoe resting on my windpipe, said,

"A little pressure and it's good night Jack Taylor."

He stood back, said,

"Just so we're clear."

I got shakily to my feet, let my head hang down as if I were still groggy. He came over, said,

"Deep breaths, champ."

My head came up fast, catching him under the chin. I followed with an almighty punch to the side of his head. He staggered back against the wall but

Managed to stay on his feet.

I went to the cupboard, poured a decent shot of Jay, knocked it back, said,

"Now we're clear."

He recovered fast, said,

"I knew it, my kind of soldier."

I said,

"We going another round or are you going to piss off?"

He smiled. I could see a bruise under his chin taking shape. He said,

"Tevis, I know he's some kind of buddy to you."

"Not my buddy."

He let out a shout, said,

"Excellent, then we have no problem."

He leaned against the wall, his body both relaxed yet crackling with a manic energy. Whatever else, I knew this guy was extremely dangerous so I decided to play along, see where the madness led. I asked,

"What exactly is it you want?"

He pondered this, then,

"Tevis is a loose cannon, probably the gay thing. He is having bouts of conscience and that I can't have."

I said,

"From what he told me, he seemed quite delighted you solved the *problem*—the guy who killed his friend."

He laughed, said,

"I like the way you tiptoe 'round the acts committed in the name of justice."

Enough of this nonsense. I said,

"So you're removing Tevis, that it?"

He made an odd sound like a strangulated sigh, said,

"No, no way."

I nodded, said,

"Great, so you can be on your way. Nice chatting with you and all that."

He said,

"You're not getting this."

"What?"

"*You* are removing Tevis from our game."

When the king is attacked by an enemy piece
We say he is in check.
The king can never stay on
or move to a square
Where he could be captured by an enemy piece.

(*Fundamentals of Chess*)

I did a background on Tevis. Didn't take long.

He was thirty-nine years old, born in Dublin, worked in IT, single. Mostly, I wanted his address.

Got that.

He lived in new apartments off College Road so I dressed like I meant business: the Garda coat, Doc Martens, black 501s, black T-shirt. I rang his doorbell. Answered with a towel in his hand and another covering his body, said,

"I was in the shower. Come in, brew some coffee, or do you want a drink?"

The apartment was completely white, even the furniture—so white you didn't want to soil it. He said,

"Sit down, chill, and I'll be ready in a moment."

I sat near a bookcase. The titles were all tech manuals, not one novel. He came back into the room, dressed in sweats, bare feet, like a guy who hadn't a care in the world, asked,

"What's up, dude?"

I said,

"Your psycho buddy came to visit."

That stopped him for a bit, then,

"And you're alive to tell the tale."

Well, there was a cue right off. I said,

"Odd you should say that as he wants me to kill somebody."

He didn't seem fazed, asked,

"Anyone I know?"

Something off about his tone. I said,

"You."

He laughed.

Not the response you'd expect. He said,

"That is priceless."

I asked,

"What do you mean?"

He gave a bitter smile, said,

"He made me the same offer."

Took me a moment, then,

"He wants you to . . ."

Deep breath.

"Kill me?"

He said,

"Guy likes to mind-fuck."

One way of putting it.

I asked,

"Are you planning to try?"

He laughed, asked,

"Are you?"

I said,

"I saved your life, what do you think?"

He moved to a cabinet, pulled out a bottle of Glenfiddich, said,

"Been saving this for a special occasion. This seems to be it."
Poured healthy measures, handed me one, said,
"To our continued good health."
I said,
"Indeed."
He knocked his right back. I paid mine a little more respect.
He said,
"Something I want to share with you."
"Go for it."
He took a deep breath, said,
"You might recall I told you my partner was killed in a gay bashing?"
I remembered, nodded. He continued,
"We'd been drinking in Jurys bar, bottom of Quay Street."
I thought,
Who the fuck drinks there?
He said,
"You're thinking who the hell drinks there."
No answer required, so he went on,
"We'd downed a fair few when I noticed a bunch of guys giving us dirty looks, like the looks you get from queer bashers."
He looked at me, said,
"Trust me, you know the hostility vibe."
I said,
"Hostility I'm very familiar with, gay or otherwise."

He considered that, said,

"The guys left before us but I knew they'd be waiting. They smelled blood."

He spat, said,

"The fuckers."

Then asked,

"Know what I did?"

I told the truth.

"Ran?"

He nearly smiled, said,

"When we came out, John didn't realize the danger and I didn't tell him. I told him I was going to grab something from the shop."

Now he paused.

He looked at his feet, as if there was some salvation there. There wasn't. He continued.

"John looked baffled, especially as there are few shops down there and even more confused when I began to walk very quickly."

Another long pause, then,

"Away."

He was now reliving it and not for the first time, said,

"I glanced back only once and they were already on him, like a pack of wolves."

A heavy silence hung over us, and finally he could bear it no longer, asked,

"What do you think about that?"

I thought of a lot of things and none of them would do him any good, so I tried,

"We all have shite we wish we could change."

As lame as it gets.

I finished my drink, said,

"Okay, what about our current situation? Maybe we should pool our scant talents and go after him."

He gave a shrill sound, said,

"No fucking way."

"What then?"

He poured another drink, sank it, said,

"I'm going to do what I apparently do best."

I waited and came the predictable,

"Run."

Our dreams drench us in sense, and
sense steeps us again in dreams.

(Amos Bronson Alcott, 1799–1888)

Dark
to
Darkest
Days
Unfolding

Trump fired his sixth top guy in so many weeks. The lunatic in North Korea daily upped his threat to fire nuclear missiles at the island of Guam. An ISIS cell led by a seventeen-year-old committed another atrocity, in Barcelona, eighteen killed, hundreds injured.

The Irish women's rugby team was beaten by France in the World Cup series, and Galway's hurling team geared up for the All-Ireland final; tickets were like gold dust.

Pat Hickey, the erstwhile head of the Irish Olympic Council, enmeshed in a ticket scandal, briefly jailed in Brazil, was now back in Ireland and declaring his aim to be reelected. You had to kind of whistle at the sheer nerve of the guy. Pictures of him in the papers told you everything you needed to understand about smugness and utter entitlement.

Our new leader, Leo Varadkar, fronted up to the UK about borders in the forthcoming Brexit negotiations. The Tories screamed,

"How dare he?"

The country said,

"Way to go, Leo."

Well, the Church, which was keeping quiet on just about every topic, reckoned a low profile might be wise, especially as one of the pope's top cardinals in Australia was arrested on child molestation allegations. His face on TV had a lot in common with the one worn by Hickey.

A book of short stories on my table had the title
How to Be a Goth in the Country.
How to resist that?
Netflix had a terrific new series, *Ozark.*
I revisited
Witnesses
The Divide
Nobel
The kind of TV that had little exposure but was true gold.

Tevis was true to his word and simply disappeared, which left me versus Michael Allen. My previous case I had with malice afterthought immersed in utter darkness, embraced revenge with total focus. If, as they say, for revenge dig two graves, then I nigh Olympic dug.

Resolved after to be done with violence, so far I hadn't as much as raised a mutilated finger in aggression.

Would it last?

Fuck knew.

When / if Michael Allen came for me, I'd react on the day and, bizarre as it seems, I didn't lose a whole lot of sleep over the prospect.

Not so much fatalistic as deep fatigued, I only knew that me and plans never met with anything like joy.

Then, life as it goes on its muddled path decided to switch from the murderous to the ridiculous. The first manifestation of this was, of course, a priest.

A very young priest.

He found me sitting on the square, watching the various encampments that sprang up overnight with a blend of refugees and homeless and stranded tourists.

The priest looked barely out of his teens and his clerical collar was blinding in its whiteness. He approached me with,

"Mr. Taylor?"

I stared at him with a mild contempt, born of years of clerical debacle. I said,

"Yeah?"

He asked,

"May I sit?"

"Kneeling would be better."

That shocked and bewildered him. He tried,

"I beg your pardon?"

I said,

"Kidding. You guys need to lighten up but, then, you don't really have a whole lot of stuff to laugh about."

He stood in a cloud of unknowing, so I said,

"Spit it out."

He composed himself as if he was about to recite a rosary, said,

"I come on behalf of the bishop-elect, Father Malachi."

I laughed, said,

"Jeez, what a mouthful."

He ventured on.

"As a mark of respect to your late mother, he would like to grace you with some assistance."

I asked,

"Money would be good, I don't have any scruples."

He faltered, then,

"His eminence would be open to offer you the position of general groundsman."

I marveled at the sheer audacity, said,

"Like the janitor."

He searched for a description, said,

"Groundskeeper would be the title."

I asked,

"Shouldn't you be saying, *His preeminence*? I mean, he hasn't got the gig yet."

He made a show of checking his watch, an impressive slim gold job, said,

"I presume you do not wish to avail yourself of this opportunity."

A hint of hard seeped into his tone and I could picture him in later years, lording it over some lofty parish. I said,

"You're in the right job, fella."

He turned to go, said,

"I shall convey your best wishes to his eminence."

I went,

"Whoa, don't do that. I didn't ask you to say it so . . . *don't*."
He shook his head in frustration, said,
"You're a very disagreeable man."
And I liked him a little better, said,
"Go preach the good word, lad."
As I watched him stride away, not a single person greeted him. In my youth, a priest took a walk, everybody saluted him.

So much had changed and utterly. I wondered how much had been lost in the new brash Ireland. A homeless guy approached and before he could ask I handed him a few notes. He was taken aback, muttered,

"You should have been a priest."

I was feeding the swans, trying not to think of my beloved dog who would always accompany me. The memory still burned hot and blistered.

The black swan glided across the basin like a sleek ballerina. I sat on the bench, which gave a view clear across the bay. You could imagine you saw the Aran Islands resting on the horizon. As America to the west wondered who Trump would rant at this day, my own day was now about to move into the realm of the absurd.

A woman in her forties sat beside me, well dressed and with a fragrance of patchouli. Not unpleasant.

She asked,

"Mr. Taylor?"

"Jack."

Got a lovely smile for that and it's amazing how such a tiny gesture can lift your deadened heart. She said,

"I've been told you have a great fondness for dogs."

What the fuck?

I said,

"I do, I did."

She pursed her lips, took a breath, said,

"Someone has been poisoning the dogs in our street."

I said,

"We can safely rule me out."

Not what she was expecting but she continued.

"I'd like to engage your services to catch the culprit."

I felt tired. A psycho was out there who waited to see if I'd kill Tevis, the two women in my life were seriously pissed at me, and now I could be a pet detective. When I didn't answer, she said,

"I can pay."

I said,

"Tell me what's been happening."

She explained how she lived in the small residential street just off Newcastle Avenue. Three of the neighbors' dogs had been poisoned, and now only four dogs remained in the neighborhood. The dogs had all been in their gardens late evening when they were hit.

I thought about that, asked,

"Any suspicions on who might be responsible?"

"No, no one has complained about dogs or anything like that."

Her name was Rita Coyne, a widow, her children grown, which was one reason her dog was so vital to her. She said,

"It's hard to be lonely when a little dog is with you."

I suggested I use her home as a base for a few days to see if I could figure out the culprit. She clapped her hands in glee, said,

"Oh, perfect. I want to visit my sister and was worried about leaving the house. Here, a spare key. I'll leave provisions for you."

I said,

"I won't need much. A chair by the window really is all."

She laughed, said,

"I think I can get you a chair."

Then gave me that look, an Irishwoman one, of *What's up with you?*"

She said,

"You strike me as a man who has simple needs."

I could have said,

Apart from

Supply of Xanax

Coke

Booze

Cigs.

But I went with,

"I'll take real good care of your home."

I asked,

"I presume you told the Guards?"

She gave a fleeting smile, said,

"They said they had more to be doing than worrying about dogs."

I nodded, not surprised, said,

"I'll see what I can do."

And, oh, fuck, she hugged me.

As I made my way back to my apartment I met Jimmy Norman, the DJ / pilot, chef extraordinaire, chatted to him about drones, which he used in his media business. Then, as I headed off, he gave me an odd look. I asked,

"What?"

He said, cautiously,

"You smell."

Very hesitant pause.

"Patchouli?"

I said,

"Old hippies never die."

He said,

"No, they usually write books about it."

Michael Allen was sitting outside the cottage he'd been allowed to use by Pierre Renaud. If he were capable of missing anyone, he might have missed the Frenchman. It was with a certain reluctance he'd taken Renaud off the board.

Renaud, more and more, had been plagued by conscience and that wasn't an option. Allen realized now that his

2

4

J

Had failed.

But he admired his noble enterprise. He was, in truth, a little tired. He considered the choice he'd given to the two *T*s:

Taylor and Tevis.

Not that he thought for a moment they'd go for that, no way, no balls.

Tevis would run and had indeed already done so. Maybe when Allen felt more energized he'd locate him, but Taylor was a whole different animal. The dude was a drunk, no mistake, but he had something, a spark, and it might be interesting to see how that could be ignited.

He went back inside, looked at his own self in the mirror, saw mostly a blank canvas. An idea was uncurling in his fevered mind, a plan that would be not only fun but a rather beautiful mind-fuck.

Moved to a large wooden table in the center of the room, unsheathed a large knife strapped under the surface, held the blade up to the light, and for a moment was mesmerized by the way it caught the light, then suddenly he struck it firmly into the very center of the table, liked the smooth motion of the action.

Repeated the motion six times and felt his mind formulate a scheme, then stopped, held himself motionless, then said in a light tone,

"A charm offensive."

Liked the sound of that.

Stood, then dropped to effortlessly do a hundred push-ups, never breaking a sweat.

He moved to the mirror, stared, still but a vague figure, commanded,

"Drop, gimme me a hundred sit-ups."

Did those with a total lack of expression, counted them off in a dead tone, bounced up, back to the mirror, shouted,

"Charm offensive."

The plank.

An excruciating exercise much favored by celebrities. He held that grueling stance for a full five minutes, stopped, took a second to orient himself, then stood again.

A local man, renowned to such an extent for making poteen that even the Guards bought their hooch from him. This morning, he had been sampling his latest batch and may have overindulged. He was now staggering close to Michael Allen's cottage and thought he heard shouting.

Heard,

"Harm offensive"?

Could that be right?

Staggered on.

Allen now moved to the mirror, saw a handsome guy begin to take shape, and allowed himself a small smile, said,

"Charmed, indeed."

The local stopped, listened, then said,
"Oh, it's *harm is offensive.*"
Considered, then said,
"Gets my vote."

Defending Against Scholar's Mate

If you are being attacked by the four move
checkmate, you need to know how to stop it.
You don't want to become a victim of this cunning
strategy. It's really very simple to prevent as long as
you pay close attention to your opponent's moves.

(Beginning Chess)

How to prepare for a stakeout. In movies they have

Doughnuts

Thermos of coffee (black)

Empty plastic bottle for pee

Fedora.

The above of course depends on the era, not to mention the ego.

Beat-up inconspicuous vehicle.

Having a house at your disposal alleviates the need for most of the above.

I had a rucksack with

Xanax

Flask of coffee / Jameson

Music

      Johnny Duhan

            Marc Roberts

                  Tom Russell/Gretchen Peters

Don Stiffe.

Good to go or, rather, sit.

I dressed in black, of course, and added a hurley as the weapon of choice.

The house was tidy, comfortable. I chose a hard back chair, placed it a bit back from the front window; an armchair would incline dozing and I wanted to be at least semialert.

I thought about who might want to poison dogs, muttered,
"Some sick bollix."

Surmised an older guy, pissed at the world, too cowardly to
confront people, so took it out on dogs.

I looked forward to meeting him.

A lot.

That first evening was quiet beyond belief, not a single suspicious character.

I was humming to myself and thought,

Humming is next to madness.

Not to mention extremely annoying. I took out the hurley,
flexed it, took a few practice swings, thought about how Galway
had reached the All-Ireland and were meeting Wexford in the
final. What I most knew about that city was it produced the
fine writer Eoin Colfer.

I played some mental chess, said,

Forks, pins, and skewers are some of the sneakiest tricks you can
use against your opponent. These tactics can lead to winning one,
maybe more, enemy pieces.

I slept most of the next day, chess pieces in the shape of dogs
running riot in my head, my daughter standing at the edge of
the chessboard saying,

"You will never hold my hand."

Woke in a shower of sweat, muttered,

"Sweet Lord."

The second night, a young couple strolled arm in arm along the street. I thought,

Young love.

They turned at the top of the street and then *came back.*

Hello?

I watched more closely. The girl was definitely peering into gardens and I knew it wasn't an interest in flowers. I just knew. A car came into the street and it spooked them. They walked quickly away.

I realized I was gripping the hurley with intent.

Third night, I was bouncing with suppressed energy, waiting.

Midnight came, and I was about to put on my headphones, sink a few Jays, and call it a night when the couple appeared.

Lock and load.

The guy was on the opposite side of the street, the girl on mine, and they were throwing items into every second garden. When the girl reached my garden I was out, fast and shouting.

Scared the living shite out of her. She actually jumped. I grabbed her roughly by the arm, the guy on the other side stared at me, then ran like fuck.

I said,

"How noble."

The girl, recovering, tried to claw at my face but I elbowed her in the gut, winding her, said,

"Now, now."

Picked up the slab of meat she'd tossed and dragged her into the house, pushed her onto the sofa, shut the door. Took her a moment, then she screamed. I picked up the hurley, gave her a wallop on the legs, said,

"Next shot is your face."

Shut her up.

She was maybe sixteen, pretty in a spoiled fashion, dressed in an expensive tracksuit. I thought,

It's always the rich kids.

I asked, holding the meat up,

"Why are you poisoning the dogs?"

She was rallying, said,

"We're giving them treats."

I smiled, said,

"Really?"

She was now gaining in confidence. I figured I'd let her run on that for a bit, asked,

"If I cook up this bad boy, you'll have no problem taking a bite?"

She gave a crooked evil smile, said,

"I'm vegan."

I moved to her, reached into her jacket, got her phone. She tried to grab it, shrieked,

"That's private, that is."

Scrolled her photos, contacts, then put the phone in her face,
a photo showing, said,
"This will be the noble lad himself."
She said,
"He'll kick your ass."
I laughed, asked,
"From a distance?"
I checked the phone some more, said,
"David Lee, well, he's left you to take the rap."
She was still thinking she had some room, asked,
"What rap?"
I lit a cig, said,
"A young child put some of your treats in her mouth and is
in the hospital so, at a guess, attempted murder."
She gasped.
"My mum will kill me."
I said,
"Tell me about the poison."
She suddenly caved, began to cry, sniffed,
"Rat poison. David said it would be a bit of, you know, drama."
I was tired of her, said,
"You can go."
"Really?"
I waved her away, said,
"Tell Dave the Guards will be in touch."

She was about to leave when she looked at me, said,

"I know you."

I shook my head, said,

"I very much doubt that."

She was certain, insisted,

"You were in the papers, saved some guy, and you're some kind of . . ."

Searched for a description, then,

"Hero."

She weighed that in her nasty little mind, then demanded,

"Give me my phone or I'll say you raped me."

Ah, fuck.

I moved right into her space, said,

"If you Google me, you'll see, among other items, I killed a girl, about your age, and guess what?"

She took a step back and I moved in tandem.

She tried, shakily,

"What?"

"They never could prove it."

She grabbed her coat, ran for the door. I shouted,

"Watch out for the dog."

In every city there are people who will hurt anyone you wish.

For money.

Galway now being a city that had our designated *hitters*.

Led by a man named Tracy, who was of mixed Brit / Irish heritage, his only allegiance being to cash. I knew him from past misadventures. Best of all, he loved dogs.

I met him in Crowes bar. He was sitting at the rear, nursing a pint of Smithwick's. He looked like an accountant, one whose books listed damage and mayhem. Dressed in a lightweight gray suit, he affected an air of bland innocence. He greeted,

"Jack, my man."

Good start.

I said,

"You look well, Trace."

You had to know him *very well* to use the derivative of his name.

He smiled at that, signaled to Ollie Crowe, who brought a pint of Guinness and a Jay chaser. Tracy said,

"Took the liberty."

We did the *Sláinte* bit, then I slid a fat envelope across the table. He raised an eyebrow. Asked,

"Personal or simply business?"

I said, simply,

"Guy who hurts dogs."

The smile was gone. He said,

"So personal, then."

I told him the saga and said I had been unable to track down David Lee. He was quiet for a while, then,

"This Lee, he *poisons* dogs?"

I nodded.

"Any reason why?"

I said,

"I'm guessing he's one of those who like to hurt animals."

Trace gave a tight smile, said,

"I'll enjoy a chat with him."

He stared at his relatively untouched pint, said,

"I drink maybe six of those, I get to the place, you know what I mean?"

I sure did.

He continued,

"Give me two shots, I'm there in like three minutes, so why delay?"

I said,

"I cover that with a pint *and* a shot."

He liked that, said,

"You always had a way about you, Jack. Not fully nuts but circling."

I said,

"I have something else but in the major league."

He looked at me, said,

"The Michael Allen psycho."

I was surprised, asked,

"You know him?"

He was quiet a bit, then,

"My trade is certainly no stranger to violence but this guy, phew. He's a whole other gig."

Meaning he couldn't help. I asked,

"Any advice?"

No hesitation,

"Shoot the fucker."

To
    fully
        appreciate
            silence
                you
                    have
to endure
a ferocious amount of noise.

                       (Michael Allen)

Galway won the All-Ireland hurling final!

The city went wild, three days of party central.

That the Irish team failed to beat Serbia in the World Cup qualifiers almost—almost—went unnoticed in our jubilation. Flush with joy and Jay, I made a last-ditch effort to salvage my relationship with Marion. I mean, if Galway took the Cup after thirty years, then surely I could win back my lady.

Met her, went

Like this.

She was dressed to dazzle, but not me, alas. We met in Jurys hotel, neutral ground, in the lounge there, surrounded by tourists asking reception why the wi-fi was on the blink. I was dressed soberly, in white shirt, funeral jacket, pressed pants, polished shoes, and massive hope.

For now.

She launched,

"I'm reconciled with my husband."

What do you say?

"Congratulations"?

Or go with your gut, go,

"Fuck it."

I lied.

"I'm happy for you."

Yeah.

She near snarled,

"No, you're not."

Okay.

I asked,

"How is Jeff, um, Joffrey?"

She actually sneered.

"You can't even remember my child's name."

Stir of echoes.

For some bizarre reason, Marion's tone of voice recalled my late mother at her most bitter. She had accused:

"You want to put me in a home."

"No,"

I'd shot back.

"I want to put you in an urn."

Marion looked at my dark clothes, not seeing any aspect that appealed.

She said,

"Try and introduce some color into your appearance. You look like something died."

Yeah, something died sure enough. Was dying and wilting right in front of her.

I said,

"Right, then, have a lovely life."

I was already walking away when she said,

"I'm happy for your wife."

WTF?

I turned, asked,

"What?"

"We ran into each other the other night. She introduced me
to her new man."

I said,

"But she left Galway."

She gave what might have been a very nasty smile, said,

"Afraid not. She seemed so lit up and you know what she
said was really great?"

Heavens, I couldn't wait to hear, asked,

"Yeah?"

She said,

"He is so good with the little girl, as if she were his."

The hits kept on coming.

I said,

"So good of you to share."

I went to the bar, ordered a large Jay, the guy there asked,

"Ice?"

I said,

"I've had enough ice in the last ten minutes to last a decade."

He placed my drink carefully before me, said,

"There's been an explosion on the London Underground."

I muttered to myself,

"The grief is endless."

He asked,

"You hear about the student in Oxford?"

No.

I shook my head, so he said,

"A homeless man asked him for some change?"

I waited.

"He took out a twenty-pound note, set fire to it, said, *Now it's changed.*"

I looked over at the Claddagh Basin, wondered how long it would take to walk over there and just fucking jump.

I drained the glass, set some money on the counter, said,

"Take it easy."

He said,

"I'm taking the plane to Australia."

I was standing outside Eason's, huge stack of Hillary Clinton's *What Happened*

On display.

Really, she had to ask?

A girl came up to me, got right in my face. I said,

"Back it off."

The dog poisoner said,

"David has got a broken arm, his face smashed, and said to give you a message."

I said,

"Make it brief."

She did back off, a vicious smile in place, said,

"He's coming for you."

Of course he was. I said,

"Tell him to join the queue."
Confused her, she went,
"What?"
I shot my hand out, tapped her lightly on the head, said,
"God bless you child."
I walked off.
She shouted some obscenity at me but it was caught on the wind, went in the other direction, much like the story of my life.

North Korea continued to launch missiles, edging closer to the U.S. mainland.
The Guards were still involved in the massive breath-analyzing scandal, where it now emerged that close to a million tests were blatantly invented. The Garda commissioner finally resigned.
You grasped for any hint of light in a world darkening by the very minute.
Took:
A homeless Irishman found dead in Manchester. Despite repeated searches, no relatives could be found.
The Met, in a compassionate move, appealed to the Irish community to attend the poor man's funeral.
They did.
In the hundreds.
Such moments gave you that breath to keep going another day.
Finding Kiki.
Like a poor version of a Pixar movie.

My daughter.

Fuck, *My daughter?*

The very words filled me with a range of emotions from joy to despair.

Me, who could barely run a cigarette lighter, was a *father.*

Then Kiki found me.

Life is trouble.
Only death is not.
To be alive
is to undo your belt
and look for trouble.

(Nikos Kazantzakis)

Kiki stood in front of me.

Looking gorgeous.

She had called at my apartment, came in, and gave what could only be interpreted as look of disapproval, said,

"Are you moving in or out?"

She had a doctorate in metaphysics, so I drew on that, asked,

"Is that a philosophical question?"

She looked like she might give me a hug. I said,

"I thought you were headed for Berlin."

She was dressed in light leather jacket, dark jeans, boots, and had the appearance of casual wealth. She said,

"That was the plan and then the most extraordinary man came into my life."

Fuck.

I asked,

"How fortunate. Are you, like, collecting men?"

Her mood soured. She said,

"No need to be jealous."

I had a hundred answers but none of them even touched on civility so I said nothing. She gathered herself together, asked,

"Would you like to come to dinner and meet him?"

Would I fuck!

I said,

"That would be just lovely."

* * *

There are times I stand on the Salmon Weir Bridge and just stare at the salmon leaping. Not that they do much leaping since the water was poisoned. But if you focus, seriously concentrate, you may, in your ideal vision, see a massive brown-red specimen jump absolutely clear of the water, and then, with a fine lunge, clear the very weir.

That delights me to my core.

A tinker woman once told me,

"Free your mind of the narrow world *amac* [son], let the wild entrance you with a magic that is not of this space."

Times I could, others I let Jameson do an artificial version, neither endured but briefly. Alongside the river are wooden seats, relatively free of graffiti and vandalism. A woman sat there, staring intently at me. I did what you do.

I stared back.

She summoned me.

I sighed, muttered,

"What fresh hell awaits me now?"

I wasn't far off the mark as it turned out.

As I approached, I could see she was in her mid-fifties, petite, with a very elegant coat that didn't quite disguise that here was a person who had recently emerged from major trauma, the stain of tragedy large in her eyes. She might be moving away from whatever it was but she certainly wasn't recovered.

I know this from bitter experience.

From such events you can put distance but, really, that's all it will be.

Distance.

She said,

"Mr. Taylor."

Patted the seat beside her.

Something in the gesture implied gentleness. Of course, it might be just an empty gesture. I sat.

She gave me a look of deep sorrow.

Up close, you could see she'd been a looker in her day but life had beaten the hell out of her. She said,

"I'm Loren Renaud."

Oh, fuck, Pierre Renaud's wife, mother of the murdered twins, and now a dead husband. The fact wasn't that she seemed beaten but that she was still functioning on any level. What did I say?

"Sorry your old man killed the kids"?

I tried,

"I am so sorry for all your . . ."

Fuck, pause.

"Grief."

She made a small sound not unlike an involuntary laugh, said,

"It seems too much for one family, *n'est-ce pas?*"

Of course, she was bound to have absorbed French. I asked,

"You wanted to talk to me?"

Long silence, then,

"You are yourself pursued by ghosts, I think."

Indeed.

I said,

"Most days I outrun them, not by much but enough to keep going."

She said,

"*Une chambre sans meubles.*"

Explained,

"My mother used to say grief is like a bedroom stripped of all furniture."

She asked,

"Would you have a cigarette?"

Now that I could handle.

Her hand shook as she took the cig. She said,

"You should have seen me a week ago."

I liked her, the bald honesty of the admission. It was simply heartbreaking.

I said,

"Been there, even my voice shook."

And she hesitated, then laughed, echoed,

"Your voice?"

"Yeah, imagine how fucked you have to be for that."

She didn't have to imagine as she still had some occupancy of that dark borough. I said,

"It is a wonder you are here at all."

And could have bitten my tongue.

She nodded, said,

"I was in a haze of booze and pills for a long time and only one thing pulled me back."

I didn't ask, waited.

She said,

"Cross my heart, I didn't know Pierre killed his . . ."

Pause.

"*Our* sons. Until the animal told me."

I had a fair idea who that was but, again, waited.

"Michael Allen. In the beginning, he was all charm and Pierre, he was in awe of him, gave him money for that ludicrous vendetta, Two for Justice, as if Allen cared a toss for that."

She gave a deep sigh, reliving many nightmares, then,

"When Pierre died, I really believed it was suicide until Allen laid out the whole shocking series of events. He told me he'd need to keep the cottage Pierre had let him use and that he would be . . ."

Deep breath.

"Requiring funds from time to time."

She gave me a look of utter outrage, said,

"In effect, I'm to support the man who destroyed my whole family."

She shook her head at the sheer horror of that.

Crunch time. I asked,

"Why have you come to me?"

She said,

"You have to stop him."
Right.

How do you dress to meet your ex-wife's new man?
Carefully.
I put on the obligatory black jacket, white shirt, tie (loosely, to suggest *mellow* or *couldn't give a fuck*), black jeans, Docs. The Docs had steel toe caps because who knows? Checked in the mirror, saw a battered undertaker's assistant, the guy you keep in the background.
Took a deep breath, a Xanax, and good to go.
We were meeting in the Bijou, a quasi-French place run by Vietnamese. Such was the mix of Galway today.
In the foyer of the restaurant, Kiki was waiting. She was looking gorgeous. Fuck it.
She said,
"My man is parking the car, we'll go ahead to the table."
My man!
Stung.
I asked,
"Where is Gretchen?"
Waited a beat, added,
"*My* daughter?"
She smiled briefly, asked,
"You are going to behave, right, Jack?"

I smiled, said,

"Of course."

We were at the table. I'd ordered a large Jay, Kiki an orange juice, when her face lit up. She said,

"Here he comes."

I turned,

Michael Allen was striding toward us.

I was utterly dumbfounded.

The bollix was smiling, hand outstretched, said,

"I feel I know you already, Jack."

Pause.

"May I call you Jack?"

He leaned over, gave Kiki a lingering kiss, said,

"You minx, you never said your *ex*"—leaned on that—"was one fine-looking dude. Should I be a wee bit jealous?"

His accent was now that polished mid-Atlantic shite that has spread like a disease. Kiki was behaving downright coquettish.

We sat, or rather they did, and I sort of collapsed into my chair. The waiter arrived, said,

"Good evening, folks. I'm Fanon and I'm going to be your server so anything you need, just holler. Now, how about drinks?"

They each ordered juice. I said,

"Double Jameson."

Allen said,

"We don't drink."

Kiki babbled on about the ambience until the drinks came, then Allen raised his juice, proposed,

"A toast to fine company."

And fucking winked at me.

They ordered some vegan shite. I had a sirloin, adding,

"Lots of heavy gravy."

Kiki excused herself to go, and it mortifies me to remember, to

"The little girls' room."

Soon as she left Allen reached over, grabbed my glass, sank the lot, belched, said,

"Christ, I needed that."

I asked,

"Won't you reek of booze?"

He looked at me as if I was completely clueless.

"Dude,"

he said.

"The chick is in love, all she smells is them there roses."

So many words there to warrant a puck in the mouth.

. . . *dude, chick* . . .

I seethed.

He said, *dude to dude*,

"Tell you, bro, I got to sneak out late evenings, after some serious fucking, grab me some carbs, like double cheeseburger, side of chili fries."

Then he looked right at me, asked,

"Tell me, Jack, that blow job she does, you teach her that?"

I was reaching for him when Kiki returned, all aglow, asked,
"You guys getting to know each other?"
I said,
"You bet."
Somehow the horrendous meal ended and I reached for the
bill. Allen grabbed it, said,
"Your money's no good with this family. Am I right,
sweetheart?"
She preened as he pinched her bum.
Outside, Kiki was getting into a cab and Allen hung back,
whispered,
"Any idea you have of, how should I say, spilling the beans,
I'll shoot the cunt of a daughter in the face."
Then he was in the cab, already fondling Kiki.

There is only one good plot. When two men want to sleep with the same woman.

(William Faulkner)

I was lost, riddled with fear, anxiety, paranoia.

Edward Lear's biographer described him as

A man who wandered hopefully

Without hope

In a desperate refusal to despair.

What in God's name was I doing reading Lear?

Shows the fragmented state of my being, that in a mad moment I thought,

Gretchen might enjoy Edward Lear.

I mean, fuck it. I had barely spoken two words to my daughter and here I was thinking what I might *read* to her. Utter insanity. At least I recognized it.

Michael Allen had my family literally as hostages and I felt powerless to act.

Pathetic.

After the wholesale violence of my previous case, I had sworn to avoid violence but now it not only beckoned but had become obligatory.

Like Chandler suggested, when you're stuck, I needed

A man to come through the window with a gun.

What I got was Tevis.

He came back.

Was waiting outside my apartment, looking tanned and healthy. I asked,

KEN BRUEN

"Couldn't stay away?"
He sighed, said,
"He found me."
I didn't need to ask who.
I did ask,
"So why are you still alive?"
He hesitated, then,
"I saw him first."
Wasn't entirely sure that was the whole story. He said,
"I was in Cork."
I echoed,
"Cork? Who hides out in Cork?"
He smiled, said,
"Exactly."
His whole demeanor was off. I asked,
"Your tan, in Cork?"
He said,
"See, thing is, Jack, not sure I fully trust you now."
I was more curious than angry, asked,
"So why are you in my place?"
He thought about that, then,
"Harley asked me to contact you."
The name struck a vague chord but evaded me. I asked,
"Who is Harley?"
"The filmmaker. He had Allen on film actually killing the
pedophile."

264

"Had? The fuck use is *had*?"

Tevis took a deep breath as if patience was necessary, said,

"He felt that if we joined forces we could finally rid all of us of Allen."

I shook my head, said,

"Tell him to bring his story to the Guards."

Got the look. He said,

"We're fucked if you don't help us."

I thought about that, then,

"Tell you what. I'll meet you guys tomorrow, see what Harley says."

If I only knew, they wouldn't be there.

In less than twelve hours they would both be dead.

I tried to ring Kiki. She had given me her mobile number. The call was answered

By

Michael Allen.

Fuck.

I asked, with more than a spread of rage,

"The fuck are you doing answering her phone?"

He made a sound I thought existed only in novels of soft porn.

"Tut-tut. Language, fella."

I tried to rein in the anger, asked,

"Can you put her on the phone?"

Long pause, then,

"Anything you wish to say to her, say to me, we share . . ."

Beat.

"*Everything.*"

I wanted to hurl the phone across the room, asked,

"Just how far do you think you can goad me?"

I heard a slight snigger, then,

"I need to ask you a biggie, my man."

"What?"

He was definitely having a high old time, said,

"I mean, old chum, I want a favor, if that's not a heavy burden on our blossoming friendship."

Yet again he blindsided me. I asked,

"You're asking me for a favor?"

"Indeedy."

I was already exhausted trying to keep pace, said,

"What."

"Would you do me, actually *us* . . ."

He managed to imbue *us* with a sinister lewdness.

"The honor of being my best man?"

Sweet Jesus.

I went,

"You're getting married?"

He gave what was meant to be a shy chuckle, a *gee shucks* sound, said,

"Why wait, when you've met your soul mate. Go for it, am I right?"

God almighty.

I said nothing.

He continued,

"Need one last teeny bit of advice, bro, and I swear I'll let you get back to your drinking or whatever it is you waste your days with."

I said,

"Let's hear it."

"It is a wee tad delicate but who better to ask than the previous daddy."

I said with absolute granite,

"Be real careful now, asshole."

"Righty-ho. Gretchen is acting more than a little flirtatious."

The sheer obscenity of that. I said,

"You are going to die slowly, I swear."

"So anyway, Jack. I'm no kiddie fiddler but it is a little awkward to keep rejecting her, um, advances."

He now sounded like a stand-up guy, bewildered by feminine wiles. I near screamed,

"She's nine years old."

That evil chuckle again, with,

"I'll do my best to end her off."

Before I could reply, he said,

"Two for Justice."

"What?"

Now he laughed loudly, said,

"The two deadbeats you sent to, um, *deal* with me? Had some car trouble, I hear."

I could hear voices behind him and he said,

"Got to run, woman to satisfy and, speaking of women, shame about the widow."

Pierre Renaud's wife?

I asked,

"You hurt that woman?"

Long beat, then,

"Grief, they say, is a bitch, am I right?"

And he clicked off.

Leaving me in a hundred different tones of dread.

I headed for O'Connell's pub on Eyre Square.

When the original owner died, she left the property to Saint Vincent de Paul. The estimated value of this was conservatively Twelve million.

Needless to say, an intricate messy legal war ensued.

I had a great affection for this bar. It was where my dad drank. Not that he ever drank anything like I did. He'd go on a Friday evening with his mates, have, at most, three pints.

He'd bring home fish and chips, in newspaper, smelling like heaven. My mother, the bitch, would cause unholy hell, roaring,

"How dare you come into this house smelling like a brewery?"

Fucking rich.

She'd have been home, sipping sweet sherry like a banshee, three sheets to the quasi-religious wind. Most times, she'd snatch the fish supper, fling it in the bin. She'd turn on me, snarl,

"What are you looking at?"

Once, I'd answered,

"Not much."

And meant it.

She'd beaten me to an inch of my life and not for the first time.

But the pub was reopened and still retained most of the character of the original, plus they drew the almost perfect pint, one that was a joy to behold, the cream top, the sheer blackness in all its pristine glory.

I was sitting on a high stool, savoring my first pint, when a guy slipped onto the stool beside me. He greeted,

"How ya, Jack?"

I nodded, noncommittal. Chat was not on my menu.

I had made a decision.

To kill Michael Allen and real soon.

The guy said,

"Not sure if you remember me. We played hurling together?"

I said,

"Oh, yeah?"

Weighing it with enough indifference to halt a Sunday Mass. Undeterred, he plowed on.

"I'm Tommy, Tommy Foyle."

I was about to shut him down when he asked,

"You ever were anointed, Jack?"

WTF?

I asked,

"You mean like the last rites?"

When I was a kid, if you heard,

"Call for the priest,"

You knew the poor fucker was a goner—not the priest, the patient.

He said,

"Yeah. I was on my last legs, and the priest came. I was never, like, real religious but when he put the holy oils on me I had such peace like you'd not believe."

I stated the obvious.

"You recovered, I see."

He laughed, said,

"I'm like a young lad now."

For a horrendous moment, I thought he said,

"I'd *like* a young lad."

I said,

"That's great."

I half meant it.

What the hell, I bought him a pint. He asked,

"Do a chaser with it?"

Yeah, he was better.

Behind me I heard a man speaking Irish, a rare to rarest thing.

He was saying,

"*Bhi fachtious orm*" (I was afraid).

I thought,

Me, too.

The other speaker said,

"*Och, no bac leat.*"

The literal translation is, "Ah, never mind him."

But you get grit behind the words, utter it with force, it's,

"Fuck him."

Needless to say, I prefer the latter usage.

I left the pub, stood on Eyre Square for a while, watching the skateboarders, and, hands down, we have the worst, the very fucking worst, boarders on the planet. Maybe it's just not an Irish thing and constant rain would deter the most ardent skater, but it was almost painful to see how downright awful they were.

Almost.

I shook myself. I had a rifle to steal.

Mysticism implies a mystery and there are many mysteries but imcompetence isn't one of them.

(Ernest Hemingway, *Death in the Afternoon*)

And in the
   Galway
      silence
         came Jericho.

A sixty-four-year-old accountant booked a room on the thirteenth floor of the Mandalay Bay in Las Vegas. He somehow managed to bring over thirty weapons along.

An open-air country and western festival was taking place below him.

He shot fifty-six dead and injured over two hundred others before turning the gun on himself. He had planned to hit fuel canisters alongside other hotels and create a fireball of epic size.

A woman in the UK used her dead husband's ashes to have a ring made so she could literally wear him.

Harvey Weinstein fled to Europe after numerous women accused him of all kinds of sexual harassment.

Catalonia attempted to declare independence and the Spanish government reacted with violence to a peaceful demonstration.

The above is just part of a daily litany of horror we were witness to in this year of our Lord 2017.

Stephen King turned seventy and had half a dozen TV and film adaptions on release.

James Lee Burke at eighty had a new Robicheaux novel published.

My mind was too fucked with rage to read but if I ever got to higher ground I had a list of old / new favorites to savor:

The Redemption of Charlie McCoy by C. D. Wilsher

Caught Stealing, Charlie Huston

A Lesson in Violence, Jordan Harper
And an old favorite from way back in 1996,
My Ride with Gus by Charles Carillo.

Such idle musings floating in my head as I side-minded the fact of having to procure a rifle and got to my apartment. There was a black envelope pinned to my door.

Black!

Now that was not going to be glad tidings.

Got inside, poured a large Jay, and carefully opened the envelope, a gold-embossed card with Gothic letters

Like this:

"Await

    the

       Dead

         of

           Jericho."

I tossed it aside, figuring I'd worry about it later.

The radio was on with the terrific Marc Roberts. He played Don Stiffe,

Followed by as near perfect a pop song as I've heard, titled "Perfect"

By Ed Sheeran.

I looked out at the bay as the song played softly behind me.

Such longing for I don't know what suffused every part of my being.

Stir of echoes.

Back in my fledgling days as an investigator, I really had no idea what I was doing.

I achieved a limited amount of success due mainly to luck, most of it bad, and sheer chance. I became friends with a Ban Garda, Ni Iomaire. To her constant annoyance, I always used the English form of her name.

Ridge.

She was a strong gutsy lady. You needed all of that to be a woman in the Guards, not to mention gay. Would that she had lived to see a female Garda superintendent. For a few years, we had a kind of embittered friendship. She did the friend bit and I supplied the bitterness.

In spades.

The third spoke in our unlikely alliance was a former drug dealer turned Zen master who made a living as a property developer. He was much closer to Ridge than I was and they both tried to, if not stop, at least regulate my drinking.

They failed.

Stewart was the first to die.

Shotgun blast to the face.

That was the beginning of the ruin of my relationship with Ridge. She reckoned I was to blame for Stewart's death and she might well have been correct but fuck if I was going to fess up. I had a list of deaths at my door as long as a Vatican rosary.

Then Ridge got killed.

Very nearly finished me off. I found myself at the end of Nimmo's Pier, mulling what the American cops describe as "Eating my gun."

Ridge at one low point in her personal life and career decided that a *straight* marriage might if not improve at least enhance both.

And what a beau she chose.

Anthony Hyphen Hemple.

I put the hyphen in there for badness.

His actual name was

Anthony Bradford-Hemple.

He was the essence of Anglo-Irish, had inherited a seat in the House of Lords,

And I think actually sat there on two occasions.

Two!

Count 'em.

Needless to say, I gave Ridge a ferocious time about all of this, calling her *Lady Ridge*. Fuck, she hated that and, in time, of course, hated me. He liked to play to the image:

Old cords, very very battered Barbour wax jacket, unkempt hair, a cloth cap, and tweeds of everything else, even his undies I'd say.

He loved *the hunt*.

Vicious fuckers on horseback chasing a poor fox.

His favorite tipple was the old G and T, Gordon's by divine right.

He'd said,

"When one is going to hounds, one fortifies with port and brandy."

Despite the above, I didn't mind him.

How Irish is that?

I tear him to shreds (much like his lot did the fox) then say I quite liked him.

He was bemused by me, utterly.

Called me

"A surprisingly well-read peasant."

For a wedding present I'd given him the collected works of Siegfried Sassoon.

Including,

Memoirs of a Fox-Hunting Man.

The one time I'd been to his manor—and I mean that in the literal sense,

Manor—

Like those of so many of the former landlords, the old house was a crumbling ruin with more ruins than people. And cold.

Perishing.

The Anglo-Irish have a thing about heating, probably due to rising costs but they seem to believe one big motherfucking log and turf fire is sufficient.

Anthony had inspected me at the door and I said,

"No butler?"

He ran with it as opposed to against me, quipped,

"When we have the poor folk over, we give the staff the night off."

Ridge had the grace to cringe.

I'd given her the full James Lee Burke set, signed first editions.

It was a time when I'd been dipping her dainty foot in the world of mystery fiction. JLB was her favorite.

Anthony took my all-weather Garda coat, sniffed at it, asked,

"Isn't this government issue?"

I gave him the look, said,

"Don't tell your wife, she's one of them."

He gave me a shocked look, thinking I meant the verboten *lesbian.*

Whisper.

I quickly added,

"One of the Guards."

Relief flooded his face, spattered with rosacea. He offered,

"Bushmills okay?"

My turn to quip.

"That's the Protestant one, give us a Jay."

I'd made a small effort, put on a Rotary tie I'd stolen from a drunk, and Anthony, surprised, asked,

"You're a Rotarian?"

Disbelief leaked all over his tone. I said,

"'Twas that or the Masons."

He let that slide, raised his glass, toasted,

"Tootle pip."

At least I think that was it, or in the neighborhood. He asked,

"You shoot?"

Like seriously?

I said,

"Only when the hurley isn't enough."

He grimaced more than smiled, said,

"Let me show you the gun cabinet."

And cabinet it was.

Stocked with enough to quell a minor peasant revolt. He picked one out, said,

"This is a beauty."

It was.

Made by Winchester, with the old bolt action. You pull that back as the bullet slides into the breech, the bolt action making a satisfying sound like the comforting clunk of your favorite old Zippo.

It smelled of oil and much usage.

I liked it a lot.

He said,

"You can fit a scope but I think that is a tad unfair to the game."

There is no answer to this that even approaches civility so I made the indifferent,

"Uh-huh."

I remember clearly holding the rifle and that freakish sense of power it falsely imparts. No wonder they talk of

"*Gun nuts.*"

Anthony was impressed, said,

"Looks good on you, my man."

I reluctantly handed it back. He said,

"We must spend a day shooting pheasant."

Later, I was outside, staring at the hill opposite the house. Ridge joined me, bummed a cig, asked,

"Don't tell Anthony."

As I lit her up, I asked,

"He'd disapprove?"

I should have paid more heed to her answer. She said,

"He disapproves of me."

She pointed at the hill, said,

"There's a fairy mound on that."

I near sneered, went,

"You believe in fairies?"

Crushing her cig underfoot, she snarled,

"I am a fucking fairy."

They were last seen westbound,
armed and dangerous.
"*Salt and pepper faggots,*" *Larkin muttered.*
"*I've said it all along. All Green Berets*
have the extra male chromosome.
"*Violence queers.*"

(Kent Anderson, *Night Dogs*)

I needed transport if I was going to burgle Anthony's gaff.

Gaff!

Christ, I had been watching too much Brit TV. I knew he had the Masonic lodge on Wednesday, and the staff (diminished as they were due to the economy) had the night off.

So it had to be a Wednesday.

I could hardly take a cab or risk stealing a vehicle. I still had plenty of cash due to Emily's legacy and the fee Pierre Renaud had given me. I went to a car rental and, fuck it, got a stuck-up gobshite in attendance who began,

"How may we be of service to *sir* this fine morning?"

Fuck, I was tired already. I said,

"For openers, don't call me sir."

That softened his cough.

A bit.

He pulled out a load of forms, said,

"If *s* . . . you would be kind enough to fill out these."

A rake of them.

I said,

"I'm here for a damn car, not a job application."

He smirked, said,

"Data protection."

Since the banks robbed us blind, data protection was the excuse of choice for laziness. But I did fill out the bloody things. Handed them over.

He scrutinized them as if they were WikiLeaks, said,

"No bank details?"

I said, tersely,

"I'm not looking for a loan, just a car."

The smirk again.

He asked, with total incredulity,

"You want to pay cash?"

His face registered that I seemed a tad old for a drug dealer. He asked,

"What size and model did *sir* . . ."

Pause.

"Have in mind?"

All my battered life I wanted one time to drive a big fucking Jeep, let out all my macho bullshit in one dizzy flourish. I said,

"Something big, like a Land Rover."

Cross my unholy heart but he actually tittered, *did* risk,

"You know what they say about men and big cars?"

God on a bike.

I leaned over the counter, got right up in his shit, as they say in the *hood*, snarled,

"You in the business of renting cars or just fucking with people?"

Frightened him. He stammered,

"No call for that," and looked around for help. There was none.

Just me.

He said,

"The Mazda is a standout in the crossover SUV class. The CX-5 is a joy to drive."

I cut him off, asked,

"Is it stick shift?"

I meant, had it gears that you manually handled so you actually knew you were doing the driving and not the automatic shite they peddled, ad nauseam, and don't even get me started on hybrids / electric crap.

He dismissed me with a shrug, said,

"Perhaps *sir would do better somewhere else.*"

The contempt dripped from every italicized word.

For a moment, I considered pucking him on the upside of his arrogant head but went with,

"You should think about working in a pharmacy. They seem to specialize in employing cunts who read you the riot act if you ask for Solpadeine."

I went down to the car park off the Claddagh and God smiled, or maybe the devil. Sitting right there was a battered Jeep, the license plates covered in dirt.

Perfect.

Took me all of five minutes to hot-wire and drive that muthah out of there.

The back window was dirty, ideal for me perch; shoot from there.

Locked and loaded.

Now I just had to break into Anthony's home and grab the rifle.

Adrenaline was giving me a jolt of energy that made me feel alive in a dark and glorious way.

Back at my apartment, I did a few lines of coke to smooth out the vibes of electricity, was watching Stephen King's

Storm of the Century,

Little realizing how utterly serendipitous that would be very soon.

A knock at the door. I opened to

Michael Allen,

Holding my daughter's hand.

He pushed the little girl toward me, snapped,

"You get her today. My love and I are having a date day."

And the fucker winked at me.

The girl looked frightened. I said,

"Come on in love, I'll get you a soft drink."

The tiniest of smiles.

How that warmed my ice heart.

Allen summoned me outside with a beckoning finger, said,

"I need a freaking day free of the damn nose snot."

Lovely.

He smirked.

"Try to keep her out of the pubs."

And he was gone.

I closed the door and faced my daughter with deep anxiety, tried,

"Anything you want to do, 'tis done."

She looked at me quizzically, asked,

"Are you, like, really my, like . . ."

Pause

". . . Dad?"

Her accent veered between American Valley girl and mid-Atlantic twang.

I said,

"Yes, I am your father."

Fuck, how weird that sounded.

She had a small satchel, made of just beautiful soft leather, *Gucci* on the front.

She took out a flask and a board game. I asked,

"Is that your tea?"

Thinking, with Kiki, it would of course be herbal green muck.

She said,

"It's a smoothie."

Right.

She looked at my overflowing untidy bookshelves, asked,

"Can I tidy that?"

OCD?

I nearly said,

"Hon, you touch my books, you lose the arm from the elbow."
But went,
"Thank you, that would be lovely."
She asked,
"Alphabetically or by genre?"
WTF?
Had to pinch my own self, mentally ask,
She's only nine?
Her little face was so elfin, so heart wrenching in its earnest-
ness, I thought of the lines of Merton,

> "*You will be loved*
> > *and it will*
> > > *murder your heart and drive*
> > > > *you into the desert.*"

Who knew?
We had an amazing day, chock-full of
Laughter
Food
Sodas
Chocolate
And
Hugs.
. . . *Hugs?*
Who could have foreseen that?
I went into the bathroom and down on my knees, whispered,

"Oh, thank you, Jesus!"

Meant it with every fiber of my wasted soul.

If you've seen series one of *The Wire* you might remember a young black drug dealer from the corner, teaching young bloods how to play chess.

In a truly fantastic, memorable scene, he demonstrates the chess pieces by calling them all the names the boys use for

Cops

Dealers

Soldiers

And explains the various moves in the way a young gun plots his way to the top.

I did that using nuns as pawns, and priests and cardinals, too, and, of course, we almost had a bishop.

The king was the pope

And

The queen, well, she was her very own mum.

She loved it and we played for hours with me promising to get a custom-made set for her own self.

A beautiful perfect day.

End of watch.

I took her hand and we stood outside my apartment, looking out across Galway Bay, my joy near boundless.

A motorbike roared behind me and I turned

Too slow.

The first bullet took Gretchen in the throat.
The second blasted through her tiny heart.
She
    emitted
        the
            tiniest
                soft
                    sigh.
And was gone.

They have a new barman
in Garavan's, but I don't talk to him at all.
In fact, most days, I stay home,
pretend to read,
the bottle at my hand
and the smashed, crushed chess pieces
at my feet. If you were to look in the window you'd
probably be struck by the utter stillness.
The absolute quiet.
You might even comment,
Jesus, a room of the dead,
but, then, you might say nothing.
Nothing at all.

Marvin Minkler was the old-school type of detective. He'd been in the army, served overseas, and then joined the Guards, progressing rapidly up the ranks by sheer smarts and that ancient concept of being good at his job.

Maybe best of all, he evaded office politics and was beholden to no one person. He'd been sent down from Dublin to investigate the highly suspicious deaths of

Tevis

Harley

Mrs. Renaud's apparent suicide

Plus the horrific shooting of a nine-year-old girl on the Salthill Promenade—the death of my beloved Gretchen. He arranged to meet me in Crowes pub, not the police station. Like I said,

Old school.

I was seated at the back of the pub where Ollie Crowe ignored my smoking as did the customers. No one approached me. Word was out about the killing of my daughter and I was best described as armed and maniacal.

True that.

Ollie had set up a fresh shot of Jameson before me, then withdrew quietly. The front door of the pub opened and a bitter November wind made a fast attempt to freeze the lounge. The man who walked toward me could only be a cop—the walk, half strut, mostly caution.

Head of snow-white hair and not because white was the new
option. Tall, in his vaguely maintained late forties. His face was
of the sort you hear called *craggy*.

Basically, no one wants to come right out and say you're an
ugly cunt.

Wearing a gray suit that was so nondescript it meant money
or poverty in that you noticed it without actually knowing why.
He held out a large worn hand, offered,

"I'm Detective Minkler. Most call me Marv. I am sorry for
your shocking loss."

I was too weary to be insulting, said,

"Jack Taylor."

He gave the hint of a smile, said,

"That much I *do* know."

He didn't ask,

"Is this a bad time?"

Every time now was a very bad time.

I kind of appreciated that.

He ordered a black coffee and asked Ollie to bring me another
of what was in my glass. I said,

"I can buy my own booze."

He nodded, fair enough, said,

"Saves me a few quid."

Quid.

His coffee came and he sipped delicately, said,

"Jeez, I could kill for a cig."

Realized his remark . . . *kill*, tried to rein it in, went,

"Fuck, that was tactless."

I stared at him, asked with a hint of snarl,

"That supposed to show you're a decent sort and like *down* with the broken sad fucker?"

He gave what could only be seen as a nasty grin and for a second, behind the outward affable manner, lurked a street cop with lots of hard edge.

I liked him a little more, said,

"You have some moves."

He relaxed, reached over for my pack of soft box Reed's, asked,

"May I?"

I said,

"Sure, need a light?"

He did.

He sat back, assessing me, then,

"Here's the thing . . ."

Pause.

"Jack.

Two young men are murdered,

Then their father hangs himself.

You save a guy from drowning,

You steal a Garda-issue coat.

A pedophile grabs your girlfriend's boy.

You rescue him.

Then the said kiddie bollix is found in pieces in a bog in Connemara."

I must have looked startled, so he said,

"Ah, you didn't know that, but to continue.

A filmmaker documenting your life and the very sad sack you saved are killed under very suspicious circumstances, and the widow of the dead father meets you, then she *kills herself.*"

He took a deep breath, leaned over, asked,

"May I?"

And took a healthy dose of my Jay.

Continued.

"Then, for fucksakes, your ex-wife asks you to mind your young daughter and she is gunned down right in front of you—the daughter, that is—and you have to wonder: what the fuck is going down here?"

I said nothing for a solid minute. I timed it, then said,

"You have one error in your account."

"Only one?"

"I didn't steal item 1834, the Garda coat."

He nearly choked, spluttered the last remnants of his coffee, gasped out,

"That's what you're focusing on, seriously? How so fucked is that?"

I signaled to Ollie who was getting more than a little pissed about all the table service, not to even mention the smoking.

I said,

"You want to know what I'm focusing on, where my ruined mind is as we speak, as the death of

Gretchen

Occupies every nightmare moment of my being, do you really want to hear what is in my mind this very moment?"

Ollie brought the drinks, did not speak.

I lifted my glass, said,

"This is what I use as a mantra to blind my mind."

Took a large swallow, lit up, then intoned in a dead fashion:

"*The window in the wall is the Sacred Host, the window between two worlds, as a window belongs at once to both the room inside and the open air, so the Eucharist belongs to both time and eternity . . .*"

Pause as I struggled for breath, then on:

"*So just as natural light comes through a window so does super-natural light come through.*"

There, I was done, madness articulated.

He looked ashen, this streetwise cop who thought he was calling some shots, and now wondered if he sat opposite a deranged individual, a man who was not only crushed and broken but had, as they say in crime novels,

Lost his marbles.

Long, tense, loaded silence, then he said,

"We arrested David Lee for shooting your girl. Seems he believed you had him near beaten to death over a dog. *A dog for chrissakes?*"

The Jay was weaving its lethal dark alchemy and I asked,

"Not a dog lover then?"

He reached in his jacket, took out one of those police-issue notebooks, and for a mad moment I regretted the loss of the career I might have had with the Guards. But it was but a fleeting dead angel, never meant to fly.

I asked,

"Ever listen to Iris DeMent, 'No Time to Cry'?"

He looked up from his notes, snarled,

"I look like a bollix who has time to listen to tunes?"

He read from the notes:

"Michael Allen, psycho extraordinary. Seems he is the root of all your, how should I say . . ."

Pause.

"Woes?"

I said,

"If you know him, about him, why is he still free and killing like he has a franchise?"

He grimaced.

"Time and time again, we thought we had enough to do him but witnesses always vanish."

I said,

"And yet he seems to do exactly as he likes."

He nodded, went,

"Even putting it to one of your old ladies."

Waited for my reaction but I was too mutilated to rise to easy bait. I said,

"Delicate turn of phrase."

He asked,

"That's it? You've gone fucking philosophical about him?"

I stood up, drained my glass, slowly buttoned the controversial coat, said,

"Leave a tip for the barmen."

He stood, contempt on his face, sneered,

"Just walking away. Hear from sources that is what you do best."

I put a rake of notes on the counter for Ollie, who nodded in sympathy. He'd heard the last comment. I turned very slightly, moved my face close to supercop, whispered,

"I'm going to shoot him on Friday, at about three in the afternoon, so you can be there to make the big arrest."

He moved back a step.

"Are you serious?"

I pondered, then,

"Maybe it's the drink talking."

Debated.

Added,

"Could be Thursday. I'm lousy with dates."

The *Sagrada Família*,
Gaudí's
temple of madness
triumph
ruin of Catholicism
monument to the greatest victory
brutal failure
breathtaking
glorious
without any semblance of order or even sanity,
but
at a certain time in the late evening,
before the revelers of Barcelona
begin to stir,
there is a profound silence
like the silence
before the bolt
on a Remington rifle is racked.

They killed the black swan.

By *they*, I mean, of course, Michael Allen.

He left the poor creature's head at my door, with a note:

"Prepare for your swan song, Taylor."

Oh, I was preparing.

Had the Jeep and on a Wednesday drove out to Anthony's mansion / stately pile, broke in easily, and stole the Remington rifle plus six long shiny bullets.

Studied Michael Allen's routine in the house he shared with my ex-wife.

How utterly fucked up is that sentence.

Every Tuesday, he strolled to the local pub, careless in his arrogance and so convinced of my cowardly acceptance of every new outrage he visited on me.

Never even gave the Land Rover a second glance.

I had the back window open and, lying prone along the backseat with a pillow as sniper's block, I watched him saunter from the house.

I think he may even have been whistling

"The River Kwai March."

I shot him first in the right knee.

Let him fall and the actual revelation of what was happening dawn on him.

I muttered,

"Suck on that."

But didn't feel a whole lot. Mainly my mind was consumed by, of all things,

Gaudí.

Yeah, as I pulled the bolt on the rifle, it gave a satisfying thud, like my favorite clunk of a Zippo.

Second shot to the gut.

They say it is the most agonizing.

He certainly roared enough. I watched,

Whispered, like a blasted prayer, a crazed mantra,

Gaudí.

"I'd go to Barcelona," I said.

Then a third shot right between the eyes.

Lit a cig with, of course, the Zip.

The door of the house pulled open and I saw Kiki run shrieking down to the piece of garbage, got in the driver's seat, and pulled away, no hurry.

I even turned on the battered radio and Jimmy Norman was reporting from, get this,

Catalonia!

If you believe in omens,

Or such drivel,

You might think it was auspicious.

I thought of Barca and Messi and the most glorious football club in the world.

Left the Jeep back where I found it, dumped the rifle in the Corrib.

Thought of the black swan, her beautiful plumage black as my heart.

I went home, made a hot toddy, it being November and the Feast of the Holy Souls.

Waited for the supercop to come get me.

He didn't.

Nobody did.

Go figure.

Mainly, I couldn't give a toss.

Next morning, I went to Annette Hynes in Corrib Travel, booked an all-expenses trip to Barcelona.

On my way home, ticket secured, I went to Dubray's book-shop, looked at an art book featuring Gaudí.

I heard a female voice say,

"Dude, you down with Gaudí?"

Turned to face a young goth woman with all that kohl eyeliner.

Jet white face, serpent sleeve tattoo, and for a mad moment I thought Em / Emily / Emerald had come back from the dead.

Shook my head, went,

"And you are?"

She said in a very Brit, upper-class accent,

"Jericho."
I nearly laughed, said,
"But of course you are."
The Jericho saga would have to hold until I had my vacation.
Don't you think?